FRANCESCA SIMON

The Lost Gods

P

PROFILE BOOKS

ff

FABER & FABER

First published in 2013
by Faber & Faber Limited
Bloomsbury House,
74–77 Great Russell Street,
London WC1B 3DA
and
Profile Books Ltd
3A Exmouth House
Pine Street
London EC1R 0JH

This paperback edition first published in 2014

Typeset by Faber & Faber
Printed and bound by CPI Group (UK) Ltd, Croydon, CR0 4YY

A CIP record for this book
is available from the British Library

ISBN 978–1–846–68566–8

FSC
www.fsc.org
MIX
Paper from
responsible sources
FSC® C020471

2 4 6 8 10 9 7 5 3 1

The Lost Gods

Francesca Simon is universally known for the staggeringly popular Horrid Henry series. These books and CDs have sold over 20 million copies in the UK alone and are published in 27 countries. *Horrid Henry and the Abominable Snowman* won the Children's Book of the the Year award in 2008 at the British Book Awards. She lives in North London with her family.

Praise for *The Lost Gods*:

'This is Francesca Simon's best book.' Amanda Craig, *The Times*

'A second hilarious story.' Julia Eccleshare, Lovereading4kids

'You have to read it: it's fast-moving, it's funny, it's silly a͏   ͏   ͏   ͏   ͏   *Th͏ B͏ k Bag*

C333547608

by the same author

The Sleeping Army

THE HORRID HENRY SERIES

Helping Hercules
Don't Cook Cinderella
The Parent Swap Shop
Spider School
The Topsy-Turvies
Moo Baa Baa Quack
Miaow Miaow Bow Wow
Café At the Edge of the Moon
What's That Noise?
Papa Forgot
But What Does the Hippopotamus Say?
Do You Speak English, Moon?

For Martin

Being famous has taken the place of going to heaven in modern society. That's the place where your dreams will come true.

Jarvis Cocker

NOTE

The Lost Gods is set in modern Britain but in a world where Christianity never existed, so people still worship the old Viking and Anglo-Saxon Gods. Time dates from the birth of Woden, 5,000 years ago.

Contents

PART I
THE GODS DESCEND

The bright, unbearable reality
when gods appear on earth
not in disguise but as themselves.

Homer

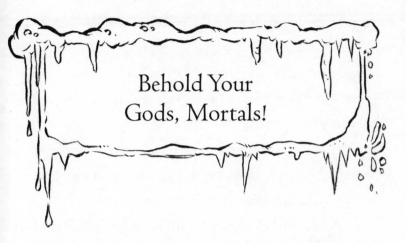

Behold Your Gods, Mortals!

Two men and a woman stood in the middle of the Millennium Bridge in the Thorsday morning rush hour, forcing the hordes of rushing London commuters to dodge round them. One wore a long blue cloak, and hid his grim face beneath a broad-brimmed hat, pulled low over his missing eye. Anyone glancing up would have noticed two magnificent ravens circling above him with easy, dipping swirls.

The other man, tall, red-bearded and muscular, dwarfed him, while the woman stood a bit apart, tossing her golden curls and scowling at the crowds pushing past her. Her nostrils quivered, as if she'd sniffed an offensive smell. The exquisite gold necklace draping her delicate neck caught the sunlight, writhing

3

and weaving in shimmering patterns over her face.

A teenage girl in stripy apple-green tights, a woollen scarf and Doc Marten boots jostled her with her backpack. The woman recoiled as if she'd been electrocuted.

'It is time to reveal ourselves,' said the one-eyed man. His rich, deep voice vibrated with emotion. 'We have waited an eternity for this moment.'

'Behold your Gods, mortals!' thundered red beard.

'Bow down and worship!' commanded the golden-haired woman.

'Move, you nutters,' muttered a workman hurrying past.

'We have returned!' boomed the man in the blue hat. 'It is I, Woden, the Father of Battles, God of Inspiration, Giver of Victory, Waker of the Dead. Tremble in awe, mortals, and worship us! ON YOUR KNEES!'

'Oh Gods, the hippie brigade on a Thorsday morning, I can't face it,' groaned a smartly dressed woman clutching two mobiles.

'BOW! WE ARE YOUR GODS!' roared Thor. 'We command you to bow!'

Two girls jogging by began to giggle.

'Move, you're blocking the bridge,' scowled a man, shoving through them.

'Weirdos,' snapped another.

'Gods, I hate street theatre.'

'Go home.'

'Bloody foreigners.'

The three Gods looked at one another. Thor's mouth gaped open.

'You are talking to Thor, the Thunder God, you worthless pieces of driftwood!' he bellowed. 'Hold your tongues, or my hammer will shut your mouths!'

Everyone hurried by a little faster, in case the madness was contagious.

'What's going on?' asked Thor. He looked suddenly shrunken. 'Why aren't they obeying? Why are they . . . *ignoring* us?'

'Why don't you look where you're going, you fat cow,' snarled a girl as she collided with the gawking, golden-haired woman.

Freyja jerked her beautiful head.

'Fat cow?' she gasped. '*Fat cow?* I am Freyja, the immortal Goddess of Love and the Battle-Dead.' Her body shook with rage. 'How dare you,' she hissed. 'I'll teach you to call me fat cow, you ugly hag. I'll turn you into a pig.' She began to mutter under her breath. 'You'll smell worse than Ulf the Unwashed.'

'I'll split open their ungrateful heads!' bellowed Thor. 'I can bring down this bridge with one blow of my axe.'

'If only,' muttered Freyja.

'Patience,' said Woden.

'Then *you* do something!' screeched Freyja. 'Show them who's boss.'

Woden drew himself up to his full majestic height. His face was cold with fury and his single eye burned. Should he smite them all? Cause the River Thames to jump its banks and sweep away this ungrateful city? Whip up the northern winds and blow down these huge halls that mortals had built to challenge the Gods during their long absence? Who did these thralls think they were, anyway? They needed to be taught a lesson.

'Pestilence and panic overtake you all!' roared Woden. 'May this bridge crumble to rubble. May you run crazed like ants escaping boiling water. May frogs fall from the sky. May you all hurl yourselves into the river and drown!'

He closed his eye and intoned a charm.

For a moment, the teeming crowds froze. Then a frog dropped from the sky and plopped onto Freyja's head.

She squealed and flailed and hurled the frog smack into the face of a passer-by, who reeled and knocked her down. She clutched Woden's tunic as she fell, tripping him and sending him crashing into Thor, as oblivious commuters, jabbering into their phones, stumbled over them.

The Gods lay prone. Freyja lifted her dishevelled head, her golden curls matted, her robes torn, her necklace glinting in broken pieces around her. She screamed and scrambled about collecting the scattered jewels. Beside her Thor groaned. Slowly Woden picked up his crumpled blue hat and placed it back on his bruised head. He was breathing hard, as if he had just run a marathon.

'That went well,' said Freyja.

'You want to marry a troll?' rasped Woden. 'Then keep talking.'

'I told you it wouldn't work,' said Freyja. 'But did you listen to me, Lord High and Mighty? Oh no, you said—'

'If you don't have anything good to say, then don't say anything,' bellowed Woden. 'It's the ill fortune of the unwise that they cannot keep SILENT.'

'What just happened?' asked Thor.

Woden shook his head.

'QUIET!' he roared. 'I must think.'

The circling ravens swooped down, perched on Woden's aching shoulders, and whispered in his ears.

Meanwhile

In icy lands heavy with frost there was a steady drip drip drip. Cracks zig-zagged across vast sheets of jagged ice. A giant glacier shuddered, split, and a huge chunk broke off and crashed with an ogre-ish scream. The surging sea exploded, lashing the frozen cliffs as more and more ice poured into the water. The cracks widened across the glistening plains.

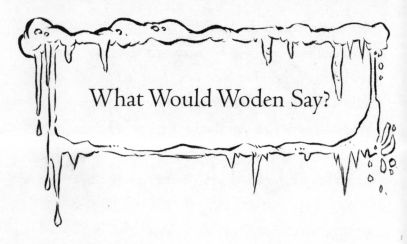

What Would Woden Say?

'Freya! Wake up.'

She'd been having the falling nightmare into Hel again.

Freya sat up, shaking. She was at home, twisted up in the blue and white duvet, looking into the sad face of the knitted snowman she'd slept with since babyhood.

Her mum squeezed her arm.

'It's over, honey. Time to get up.'

'Was I screaming?' asked Freya.

Clare raised her eyebrows. 'No louder than usual.'

Half an hour later, Freya sat at the table and ate her cornflakes. Her mum bustled round with her phone under her chin, making Freya's lunchtime herring sandwiches while trying to sort out the Fane cleaning rota and the food for Woden's forthcoming festival. Freya watched as Clare added lettuce to the sandwich. Once Freya would have objected, and sulked if she thought she'd get away with it, but her food fussiness had vanished since her 'return'.

That's how her nine-day disappearance last spring was referred to. She'd been 'gone'; then, thank the Gods, she'd come back. 'Concussed,' the doctor at Baldr's hospital had said, as if that explained everything.

Did it? Sometimes Freya wondered. It was a convenient excuse, which explained nothing about what had happened to her. Sometimes, when it all seemed most dream-like, she'd go to the Clark's shoebox she kept hidden at the back of her wardrobe and pull out a thick stack of yellowing newspaper clippings. For a few days she'd been headline news:

EVENING STANDARD

FREYA IS ALIVE!
MUSEUM MYSTERY DEEPENS

Missing schoolgirl Freya Raven-Gislason was found earlier today wandering in a confused state by Woden's Temple, near the spot she was reportedly seen nine days ago with two teens in fancy dress. She was bruised, dehydrated and suffering from exhaustion, but otherwise in good health.

Police are continuing their search for the four stolen chess pieces from the priceless Lewis hoard, which vanished from the British Museum last week. A King, a Queen, a Berserk, and a Knight's horse are still missing. Police would only confirm that Ms Raven-Gislason was helping them with their enquiries.

Sunil, the policewoman who first found her on the Millennium Bridge had been kind but insistent. Had she seen who'd stolen the chess pieces? Had *she* stolen the chessmen? No, Freya had said. They stole me, more like, she'd thought.

Had she run away from home or been kidnapped? And what of the two oddly dressed teenagers she'd been seen with on the bridge? Did she know them?

No, she'd said. That wasn't entirely a lie: how could she claim to *know* Alfi and Roskva, mysterious beings from another time and place?

Sunil had persisted: 'Around the time you were seen on the bridge, there was another incident involving a man wearing a bear skin attacking several cars on Upper Thames Street with a sword. A number of people were injured, some seriously. Did you see this man?'

'No,' lied Freya. Silently she'd wished the policewoman good luck trying to arrest Snot. They'd pressed her and pressed her to say where she'd been. When she told them she'd been to Asgard and Jotunheim and Hel, and met the Gods, her mum had intervened and insisted they take her to hospital and get a lawyer if Sunil was going to accuse her daughter of theft. Freya was frightened she'd be arrested, but after the initial questioning, she was never summoned to the police station again. Everyone just treated her like a runaway, and that was that.

Beneath the cuttings, Freya kept a handful of business cards, from all the journalists who'd jostled for exclusive interviews, and the publicists who'd begged to represent her and sell her story. Clare was adamant that Hel would warm up before Freya sold a story to the newspapers, or even spoke to journalists, and Freya had been so bewildered and in shock after her return she hadn't known what to do, so she did nothing.

Eventually, interest died down. People still occasionally pointed at her in school, and whispered about her behind their hands, but that she could live with.

What was hard was that there was no one, absolutely no one, she could tell her story to. Who'd believe her anyway – that she'd been to Asgard, rescued the Goddess Idunn from Hel and restored the Gods to youth? She wouldn't believe anyone who said that, so why should anyone believe her?

Safer to say nothing.

Buried at the very bottom of the shoebox were Freya's greatest and most hidden treasures. An arm bracelet, heavy with gold. Thor's gift to her, when she left Asgard. Alfi's metal brooch, intricately carved and twisted. Freya held them, her hands trembling.

And a single falcon feather, tucked inside an old leather glove.

Freya picked up the falcon feather and shook it. The feather shimmered and became a translucent falcon skin cloak. Freya touched the silky feathers and shook it again. The way it shrank back immediately to a single one always awed her. The tail feathers were still singed from the fire which had almost engulfed her when she'd spun into the citadel of the Gods, hunted by the eagle giant Thjazi.

Whenever Freya thought she must have dreamt the whole thing, she'd take the feather and shake it out into the glowing falcon skin. Once she'd been tempted to put on the cloak of feathers and take flight, but fear held her back. That, and the nightmares.

The falling nightmares were the worst – where she tumbled into Hel again, down down down into the freezing blackness where Loki waited to trap her and Thjazi, with his rushing wings and outstretched talons, ached to rip her to shreds. She'd be walking down the street, or queuing at the post office, and without warning she'd feel herself swept into a whirling vortex again and feel so dizzy she'd have to run out and get some air, and reassure herself that she was back in Midgard, and safe. She was still worried that, somehow, Loki would find her and take his revenge. But six months had passed, and he had not appeared. Sometimes Freya felt a prickling certainty that she was being followed, but whenever she spun round, no one was there.

'You really should be making your own lunches now, you know,' said Clare.

Freya snapped out of her reverie.

'What?'

'I said you're old enough to be making your own sandwiches,' repeated Clare.

'I did offer,' said Freya.

Actually, she liked having her mum make her lunches. It made her feel taken care of. Clare used to run her baths for her, squeezing in just the right amount of bubble bath, but she hadn't done that for a while, not since the divorce. Freya had done it for Clare once, when she was little, but Clare screeched that she'd put in far too much bubble bath and the suds had overflowed the tub, so Freya hadn't done it again.

'What would Woden say?'

Oh Gods, not a sermon. Who'd have a priestess for a mother?

'He'd say, "It is good to rely on yourself." Don't cast Woden's words to the winds.'

'Yes, Mum,' said Freya. It was always best just to

agree with Clare and get it over with. Thank Gods, thought Freya, today's sermon was brief. Sometimes Clare would get carried away and lecture her for ages.

Now was as good a time as any to raise the subject of Hel's shrine. How did you make a shrine to one of the Gods? Pile up a few rocks in a sacred place somewhere? Did she need a priest to bless them? What charms should she recite? She'd promised Hel, and had done nothing. A shrine to the Goddess of Death. Freya shuddered. But a vow was a vow.

Freya opened her mouth to speak, and the conversation she was about to have with her mum passed silently through her mind.

'Mum, I want to build a shrine.'

'Darling, that's wonderful. I knew you'd start taking an interest. Right, I can suggest several places where Thor needs—'

'It's not to Thor.'

'But He's your protector God. Your first shrine should always be to your protector.'

'This shrine is to Hel.'

Then Clare would fix Freya with *the* look, as if to say, I saw your lips move and heard your voice say something, but I absolutely cannot believe the words that just came out of your mouth so I won't.

'Did your father put you up to this, Freya?' Clare would say. 'Because it's not funny. That is slander against the Gods.'

'It's nothing to do with Dad,' she'd reply.

'Freya, you've been behaving strangely. I think you should see a doctor . . .'

And before Freya could say anything more she'd be bundled off to the GP, who'd refer her to a psychiatrist, and there'd be endless worried conversations about all her dark thoughts . . .

Perhaps, thought Freya, it would be better to google 'How to build a shrine to the Gods', and then find a secret spot on Hampstead Heath and create it there. Or in a little corner of Highgate Cemetery, tucked away among the grave mounds. What was one more secret, among so many?

The *Today* programme on BBC Radio 4 was on in the background. Clare liked listening as she bustled around getting ready for work.

'Well we have Thor to thank for the stormy skies all over the south-east today,' said BBC newsreader Zeb Soanes. 'The unseasonably frosty autumn weather is continuing throughout the British Isles.

The worst weather will be in Scotland with thundery showers and the risk of flooding across the region lasting through Fryggday . . . boy, what has Thor got against the Scots?

'Coming up: Woden's ravens leaving the Tower of London for the first time in history – coincidence or bad omen – email us and tell us what you think. And, while Europe continues to be blanketed in snow, we'll be talking to scientists who report that the progressive shrinking of the Arctic sea ice is bringing colder, snowier winters to the UK and other parts of Europe, North America and China.

'First, what the papers say. The *Guardian* leads on "NHS crisis as cuts bite" while the *Daily Mail*'s headline is: "So much for global *warming* – September shaping up to be the coldest in 200 years."

'Cold? Huh. Try Jotunheim if you want cold,' muttered Freya.

'What?' said her mum.

'Nothing,' said Freya.

'. . . while *The Sun*'s lead story is "Pay up, scum! 87% of *Sun* readers demand that compensation for robbery and unlawful killing be increased", while the *Telegraph* goes with "Queen leads tributes to her ancestor,

Woden, in victory celebrations at the Cenotaph".

'Fane attendance is down to its lowest level since records began, and fewer than 1% of the population now attend Sunday worship. In our studio today we have the Archpriest of York. Welcome, Archpriest. To put it bluntly, is the Wodenic faith finished in Europe? Why do you think religion plays such a small part in people's—'

Clare switched off the radio.

'He's not telling me anything I don't know,' she said.

'You're doing a great job, Mum,' said Freya.

Clare sighed. 'Yeah, well, I try. How long I'll *have* a job is another matter. When it is fated that . . .' She didn't finish her sentence. 'Anyway, I'll be a bit late tonight, will you be okay on your own?'

'Yes,' said Freya. She rolled her eyes. She'd been to Hel and back, she could be alone in her own home for a few hours. Honestly. Mum still thought she was four years old.

'I've got the Youth Choir practice . . . you don't want to come, do you?'

'No,' said Freya. 'Sorry. Too much homework.'

Her mum was always trying to drag her into Fane

activities. It was bad enough that Clare forced her to attend Fane every Sunday when she'd so much rather sleep in or watch telly.

'If you ever change your mind, we could really use some extra bodies,' said Clare. 'Could you ask around at school?'

'Okay Mum,' agreed Freya. As if she'd spend her time recruiting for her mum's choir. She was considered enough of a weirdo already, without have the Gods-squad label stamped on her back.

'Make sure you wear an extra jumper,' said Clare, gathering up her papers, 'it's cold outside.'

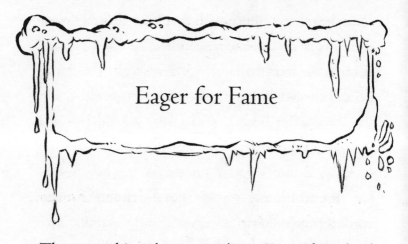

Eager for Fame

The worst thing about attending a Fane of England secondary school, thought Freya, *the very worst*, was the daily RE assemblies which went on forever, led by the dour school priest, Ivar Fairhair, the most boring man in Britain. While Priest Ivar droned on, her fingers itched to get out her mobile and check for text messages, but if she was caught she'd be in big trouble.

He was in particularly grim form this morning. 'Everyone must endure the ending of life in this fleeting world. The only thing which never dies is renown for noble deeds. As Woden the All-Father teaches us, "We are all mortal. Yet words of praise will never perish, nor—"'

To block out his monotone exhortations, which

she'd heard a million billion times before, Freya read the nine commandments carved in painted gold letters into the large wooden scrolls that hung behind the head's lectern.

The Nine Commandments

1. We are the Lords your Gods. Thou shalt have no other gods before us
2. Thou shalt remember the Gods' feast days
3. Thou shalt not slander the Gods
4. Thou shalt not steal
5. Honour thy children for they alone will carve thy name upon the gateposts
6. Thou shalt not kill. Murder leads to blood feuds
7. Thou shalt offer hospitality to strangers
8. Thou shalt not bear false witness
9. Thou shalt not covet thy neighbours' gold hoard, nor any thing which is his

Now it would be, 'don't covet your neighbours' telly, or her designer handbag, or his flash car'. Freya didn't care at all about handbags, but thought she'd quite like to covet a gold hoard. Those old commandments just put ideas into your head, she thought, and then blushed, and was glad no one here could read her thoughts.

Unlike Woden. She'd hated that he'd been able to see inside her head. Thank the Gods no one else could.

'And what is Woden's nature?' rumbled the priest, making her jump.

Grumpy, thought Freya.

She was the one who'd actually met the Gods. So far as she knew, the only human who had for centuries. But no one would ever believe her, so she kept quiet. It was tough though, when priests talked as if they knew the Gods personally, and were so quick to say, 'Woden would want you to do such and such,' and 'Frey, full of grace, brought you prosperity . . .' Then she'd think, 'If you only knew . . . you think you're such a smarty-pants when in fact . . .'

It was hard to keep so big a secret, even harder not to boast about what had happened. But Freya knew if she breathed one word she would be ridiculed. Even her best friend Emily knew nothing. Sometimes having secret knowledge you couldn't share was worse than knowing nothing.

'The All-Father is Lord of Poetry,' intoned Priest

Ivar. Oh Gods, when would he finish? thought Freya. 'He is so fair and full of majesty that all the Gods who sit with him in Asgard quail in his presence. As the prophet Snorri declares, "He is the cleverest of all the Gods, and from Him all who are inspired learned their art and skill."'

Hmmm, thought Freya, wonder how inspired they'd all be if they'd seen him as a tottering ghost like I did?

'Now, what are Frey and Freyja's attributes? As the prophet Snorri writes . . .'

Her fellow students shifted restlessly around her. No one, even at a Fane school like hers, paid much attention to all the Gods talk: most of them only pretended to be religious to get into the Fane school because it got better results than the comp down the road. Religious chatter was just so much background noise while people got on with the important things in their lives like comparing mobile phones, watching reality TV shows, and discussing which celebrity had the most cellulite.

*

Mr Borg, her Citizenship teacher, stood in front of the white board, marker in hand. This was her least demanding class, a bit of discussion at the end of the day. Easy to daydream in.

'Right, everyone. Let's share career ambitions. Grisla, you start. What do you want to be when you grow up?'

'I want to be famous,' said Grisla, giggling.

'Excellent,' said Mr Borg. 'You should all be eager for fame. Famous for what?'

Grisla looked blank.

'Famous for great deeds? Famous for accomplishments? Famous for—'

'Famous like on telly,' said Grisla.

'Okay, how many of you want to be famous?' asked Mr Borg.

Every hand shot up.

Freya put her hand up then slowly put it down. What was she thinking? She'd had her brief brush with fame when she'd returned from her 'disappearance' to the flurry of media interest and everyone thinking she'd either been kidnapped or run away. That wasn't the kind of fame she wanted.

Her friend Emily shot her a quick glance. Freya raised her eyebrows and grimaced.

Of course she'd love to be famous. But famous

in the fun, celebrity way, wearing gorgeous clothes, living in a fabulous house and going to swanky parties. Not the infamous of people whispering about her and thinking she was a liar and a thief.

Mr Borg caught Freya's eye. Please, please don't call on me, she thought.

'My question remains, what do you all want to be famous *for*?' asked Mr Borg. 'Famous poet? Famous scientist? Famous teacher, anyone? Who wants to be a good actor or run a successful business or be a talented chef? No one? Will only being a *famous* actor or a *famous* businesswoman or a *famous* chef do?'

Duh, thought Freya. Mr Borg was an idiot.

'Freya? How about you? What do you want to be famous for?'

Freya shrugged. She wanted to be famous for *being*, not famous for doing.

'Just famous,' said Freya.

What Bad Fate Was Hers?

Freya let herself into the empty house, stamping her feet to warm up and dumping her heavy coat over the bicycles that cluttered up the hallway. I'm a latch-key kid, she thought. That was supposed to be a sad thing, but she always liked having the place to herself. She could blast her music as loud as she wanted, drink milk from the bottle if she felt like it, sneak a bag of crisps, watch rubbish telly and not do her chores. The moment Mum spotted her, the inquisition would start: 'Have you done your homework? How was the maths test? Why haven't you put away the laundry? Did you write and thank Granny for the birthday cheque? You haven't? What would Woden say?' Sometimes Freya regretted leaving her bedroom; at least there she was safe from being hassled.

28

She and Clare had stayed in the small North London terraced house near her mum's Throng after her parents got divorced. Now her dad, when he wasn't away working in Dubai, rented a tiny flat nearby converted from a disused Fane, which was ironic considering how much Mum deplored how many old fanes were being deconsecrated. Or maybe that was why he'd done it. Freya tried to stay out of their sniping fights.

Right, she thought, walking down into the untidy kitchen, still piled with the breakfast plates and the remains of yesterday's dinner. She and her mum had a long-standing unspoken war to see who could leave the dishes lying around the longest without washing and putting them away. Clare usually cracked first.

Yummy chocolate biscuits first, then she'd check Facebook and ring Emily to make plans for the party at Jenny's and to find out who she was voting for on *Strictly Come Baking*. You were supposed to be 13 to have an online profile, but she would be, soon enough, and everyone she knew was on it, so no big deal. Just so long as her parents didn't find out, because then it suddenly would be a big deal.

What they don't know won't hurt them, she thought,

making herself comfortable at the rickety wooden kitchen table, pushing aside the stacks of letters, Fane leaflets, and books littering it. There's so much my parents don't know, anyway. She looked around to see if Clare had left one of her bossy notes, detailing all of Freya's unfinished chores and what she needed to do before Clare got home. No note, just a copy of the Fane magazine, open to the forthcoming events page, written in her Mum's usual upbeat, exhorting style. Freya read it idly while munching on her biscuits.

The traditional procession of the Idols of Woden and Thor and Freyja and Frey and Tyr will take place next solstice to celebrate the Feast of the Unconquered Sun, and it would be great to have a big turnout to follow the cart as it travels through Holloway. We'll be setting off at 1:30 pm from our Fane and walking in a circle. The cows will be hitched at 12:45 and anyone who wants to help decorate our cart the day before is welcome. Children are urged to come dressed up as their patron God – or perhaps as the Wolves who try and fail, thank the Gods, to swallow the sun and moon – and there will be a prize for best costume. Our hospitality committee will be providing tea and biscuits back at the Fane when the cart returns.

Remember to sign up for our annual pilgrimage to Woden's temple at Uppsala. And of course, the Fane flower rota needs more volunteers. Please email or—

The doorbell rang.

Oh Gods, it'll be someone trying to get me to sponsor them for their charity run, thought Freya. Should she pretend she wasn't home and not answer it?

The bell rang again, loud and insistent. Freya flung open the front door.

'I've already spons—'

Two people pushed their way into the narrow hallway and slammed the door behind them.

'No!' screamed Freya.

The one-eyed, craggy-faced man glowered at her beneath his battered blue hat. The golden-haired woman held up her clenched fists as if to strike her.

Freya backed away, crashing into her bicycle, which toppled over.

31

'NO!' she screamed. 'I went to Hel for you. I restored your youth. I was almost eaten by a dragon and ripped to shreds by a giant. I've done my bit. Go *away*! *Please* go away. You don't belong here. Please.' Her breath came in harsh pants.

Why couldn't they leave her alone? Hadn't she done enough?

The one-eyed God looked down at her coldly. His head nearly touched the low ceiling.

'That is how you greet your Gods?' said Woden. 'Are you eager to enter your grave mound? I've killed people for less . . .' He fixed her with his dark, terrible eye.

Freya cowered in the narrow hallway and stared at the Gods. Their robes were torn, covered in mud and dirt. Their faces were bruised and scratched. Freyja had muddy footprints on her tunic and her golden hair hung in snarled knots. Woden's single eye was swollen.

'Lords,' whispered Freya, swallowing. She bowed her head. 'What are you doing here?' Her heart was beating so fast it was difficult for her to speak. She felt sick. 'I did what you asked . . . I brought back Idunn and her golden apples, you are all young again . . . why are—'

Woden glared at her.

'We, the sacred people, do not answer questions, we ask them.'

Freya shrank back against the stairs.

Maybe the Gods just had a little question or two for her, and then they'd go back to Asgard, no harm done. Maybe they were just checking how she was, a social call. Yes, a friendly visit, to thank her, finally, for saving them and restoring their youth. Thanks for all she'd done for them had been sparse, Freya recalled.

'Please come in,' she said, wishing her voice sounded stronger.

The Goddess snorted. 'I wondered when you would recollect what is owed to guests,' she said. She looked around the small house as if she were surveying a stinking pigsty. Her nose crinkled.

Freya opened the door to the small sitting room, and stood back while the two Gods entered. The worn wood floor trembled beneath their feet.

BANG! BANG! BANG!

The knocking was so loud it sounded like the door would shatter.

'Answer it,' said Woden.

Freya felt faint.

She pulled open the door and a red-bearded giant limped past her, knocking into the hall chandelier and sending it swaying back and forth and smashing repeatedly into his head until he tore it off the ceiling and flung it to the floor. Thor tried to lift the hammer he was dragging behind him before lowering it and breathing hard, as if the weight had been too much to bear.

'Where are they?' he growled.

Freya squeezed against the wall and pointed to the sitting room. Thor stomped in. Freya heard the sound of splintering wood and another crash.

Oh my Gods. This wasn't happening.

She peeked round the door to see Thor kicking away the pieces of the wooden chair he'd shattered. Freya winced. That chair had belonged to her gran. Thor moved to the dusty green sofa beside the Goddess Freyja, squashing her as his huge body took up most of the space. The battered couch sagged alarmingly under his weight. Freyja's plump lip quivered as she perched cautiously on the sofa's edge, avoiding the flat throw cushions. Freya could see a tomato stain on one from the pizza she'd secretly eaten in front of the telly the night before, as her mother forbade her to eat in the sitting room. The Goddess gathered her tattered robes tightly around her.

'I saw no offering to the Gods outside your doorway,' she said. 'I'd have expected at least a cow.'

'Offering?' said Freya.

'Where is your mother's loom?' continued the Goddess.

'No loom,' said Freya. Clare could barely sew on a button.

The Goddess's beautiful glacier-blue eyes widened.

'No tapestries. No gold or silver,' she muttered, as if taking an inventory. 'And where is your sleeping bench?'

'We have two bedrooms upstairs,' said Freya.

'And where are your pigs and chickens?'

'We don't—' began Freya.

'Enough with your inane questions,' snapped Woden. 'They change nothing.'

'This is a dump,' muttered the Goddess. 'When I think of my beautiful hall Sessrumnir in Asgard . . .'

Woden remained standing. Freya, unsure what to do, stood also. What bad fate was hers? Should she offer them some biscuits? A cup of tea? Crisps? What did Gods eat, anyway?

Woden looked around her sitting room, with its orange Ikea armchair and the faded yellow and brown Turkish rug. The room felt tiny with these giants in it.

'Your hall is bright,' he said. 'But where is your hearth?'

Freya swallowed. 'We don't have one, we have central heating,' she said. 'It's on at the moment, even though it's September, because it's so cold outside.'

Woden touched the radiator, then leapt back.

'The metal is hot to the touch,' he murmured. 'Yet I see no fire or heated stones.'

Thor grunted. 'Dad, get on with it and stop wasting time,' he growled. 'We can explore Midgard later.'

Woden sighed.

'So much time has passed since we last visited Midgard, this shrouded world I created with my brothers,' said Woden, 'and everything has changed. I do not recognise my creation. While Asgard has been frozen in time, Midgard has moved on. The dwelling places of men, their chariots, their halls, their garments, all has changed.' He shook his head. 'I granted them boldness and wisdom, and I marvel at what they have created. They have made roaring metal tubes which fly without a falcon skin. How did they discover such magic? They have light and heat without fire. Their towns are monstrous and filled with trollish screeches. It's a strange new world we have awoken to. At least there is still war.'

'That's *one* good thing,' said the Goddess Freyja. 'Plenty of fresh supplies for the Choosers of the Slain to bring back to Valhalla.'

Freya looked carefully at the Gods. Last time she'd seen them they'd been dying, tottering ghosts, clothed in fluttering rags. Now they were young again. Their cloaks and tunics were weird, about 5,000 years out of date, but then what could you expect? What in the name of the Gods were they doing in her sitting room? They should be in Asgard, not here in London plonked on saggy sofas and scowling like sulky teenagers sitting on a wall outside an off-licence.

Then, remembering that Woden could read her

thoughts, she blushed and looked away.

The Goddess Freyja clicked her spectacular necklace of twisted gold, frowning. Thor looked out of the bay window and drummed his fists on his muscular legs. Was it her imagination, or did they seem strangely reluctant to speak?

'We don't want to be here in Midgard,' said Woden after a long silence. 'Asgard is our home. But we are . . . desperate.' He winced.

Desperate? That was a shocking word for a God to use. Freya could not hide her astonishment.

'Our worlds are in danger. Grave, terrible danger,' said Woden. Freya felt chilled. She chewed on her sleeve. The ticking of the old carriage clock on the mantelpiece suddenly sounded very loud. 'We would not be here otherwise.'

Why did I have to let them in? thought Freya. Why of all days couldn't I have been somewhere else? I should have gone to Mum's Fane choir.

'Your fate catches you wherever you are,' said Woden sharply. 'Listen carefully.'

Must I? thought Freya. She'd learned the hard way that whenever Gods ordered her to listen, it was to tell her things she didn't want to hear.

Next Time You Create a World, Do It Better

'Long, long ago, in the age of Ice, frost giants trampled over the earth, which we had formed from the body of Ymir, the forefather of all giants,' said Woden. 'We defeated those evil destroyers, and buried them deep in layers of ice and frost, tightly bound in frozen fetters. But now the glaciers are melting. Drip. Drip. Drip. The frost giants are stirring and breaking free of their icy bonds. Once they are free they will march here, slicing through the land to reclaim their kingdom. Thrym. Fornjot the Destroyer and his fearsome offspring: Jokul the glacier. Jarnhaus the Iron Skull. Kari the north wind. And countless others. The giants are unleashing their fury, howling for vengeance against Gods and men. This world will once again be burning ice, bitter winds, and biting flame. 'Can't you smell them?' He sniffed. 'The ice in the evil air.'

The Gods shuddered, as if trolls had trampled on their grave mounds.

Freya thought about the freezing cold summer, the freakish storms, the pictures of polar bears clinging to tiny shards of icebergs, the eerie sounds of cracking ice.

The murderous giant Thjazi, who'd so nearly killed her, flashed into her mind. She flinched.

'Why don't you fight them? You're the Gods. You can't let the world freeze over.'

Woden's baleful eye blazed.

'We have made a tactical retreat.'

Freya gasped. 'You've *run away*?' This was getting worse and worse.

'I said, a *tactical* retreat,' roared Woden.

'You talk too much, mortal,' snapped the Goddess.

'The battle-brave warriors of Asgard, the fallen heroes, the Einherjar, will fight them first,' said Woden. 'Shields will be split. Swords will gnaw like wolves through armour. But alone they will be helpless before the might of the giants.'

What was he saying? That the Gods had

abandoned Asgard and Midgard to an army they knew could never win? Freya thought her head was going to explode with dread.

'You said you defeated the frost giants once before,' said Freya. Her voice quivered. 'So why don't you do it again? Why aren't *you* stopping them?' What are you doing in my sitting room when you should be defending Asgard? she wanted to scream.

'Tell her,' said Thor. Freya was shocked to see him brushing away a tear. His gigantic fist clenched his hammer.

The Goddess rolled her eyes as she nervously clutched and unclutched her ringed hands.

'As you can see, our youth is restored,' said Woden. Freya waited for the 'thanks to you', which didn't come. 'But our divine power has not returned. Thor can barely lift his hammer. Heimdall cannot hear the grass growing or fish breathing. I cannot see into the future, or raise the dead. I cannot even paralyse my enemies in battle or blind them. With the last of my strength I tried to sow panic on the bridge between our worlds this morning, and . . . did not succeed. I can't even turn into a hawk or a boar any more.'

'Our strength kept our enemies bound; our weakness has released them,' growled Thor. His face flushed an angry red.

'But I don't understand,' said Freya. '*Why* are you weak?'

She had a sinking feeling she didn't want to hear the answer. What did their troubles have to do with her? Let them find someone else for once, she thought fiercely.

'It seems we need—' Woden's brow furrowed as if he had just waded through sewage '—the worship of the sons and daughters of men.'

Thor and Freyja wrinkled their faces in disgust and horror.

'This is so demeaning,' muttered the Goddess. 'So inglorious.'

'But you are still worshipped,' said Freya. 'My mother is your priestess. The Queen of England is head of your Fane. Britain is a Wodenic country. I go to a Fane school. Want me to recite the nine commandments?'

'NO!' said Woden.

'Be quiet, you ugly herring,' hissed Freyja. 'The All-Father is speaking.'

Freya resisted the urge to stick out her tongue at the snapping Goddess. Why oh why had she been named after such a mean shrew?

'I've sent my ravens far and wide to bring me news of what this world we created so long ago has become,' continued Woden. 'And what I have learned is that we are no longer woven into its warp and weft. How could this happen? Why has this happened? There is no fervent hum of worship and love and fear, no stream of savoury sacrifices reaching our nostrils. Our idols and temples are neglected. We are rarely in people's thoughts. During our long absence, for reasons I do not understand, mortals began to live without us.'

'The ungrateful trolls!' spat Freyja. 'After all we did for them, this is how they thank us? They never pray, they never sacrifice, they—'

'We never gave the children of Heimdall much thought,' interrupted Thor. 'So long as they worshipped and built temples and brought offerings, all was well. We gave them good harvests – mostly – wealth to the lucky few, Valhalla for the brave, the chance to win glory which alone outlives death, victory to one side or the other in battle, and everyone seemed happy with the arrangement.'

'Actually, I blame you, Woden,' said the Goddess. 'Next time you create a world, do it better.'

Woden glared at her.

'You think you're so smart let's see you try it.'

'I still can't believe we have to kowtow to mortals,' said the Goddess, flicking her hair and glaring at Freya. '*So* beneath us. How did we ever give the driftwood such power over us? Humans are so frail, so fragile, so momentary, and the Wolf and the Snake can swallow them all – and yet only their worship makes us truly divine. Aaarrrghhh! It seems we are fated to n-n-need them,' she added, stumbling over the word.

You'd think she was saying she needed a head transplant, thought Freya angrily.

'Gods without worshippers are just legends. Nothing more,' explained Thor. He looked woefully at his hammer, trailing on the floor. 'Fate is harsh.'

'*We* will not dwindle to stories told round a hearth fire,' said Woden. 'We have seen off other gods, false gods, those Greek weaklings – ha. And don't get me started on those Roman and Egyptian sons of mares . . .' He snorted and his one eye blazed.

44

'Jupiter. Minerva. Osirus. Amun-Ra. They're all sleeping with the trolls now. Our Temples built on top of theirs, as they should be.'

Woden glared fiercely out of the window, as if seeing his mighty Temples looming above Jupiter's crumbling stones.

'But now *we* are weak,' whispered Woden. 'We are lost Gods. We need worshippers. Lots and lots and lots of worshippers. We NEED to be revered and feared and idolised, and for our names to be on everyone's lips and engraved upon everyone's hearts. You must help us regain our followers. Once we recover our divine strength, no frost giants can withstand us. You will be our guide to this strange new world.'

The three Gods looked at her expectantly, as if all she had to do was open the door and a stream of devotees would pour in. Freya stared at them, open-mouthed. Were they mad? Had they lost their minds as well as their powers?

'How am *I* supposed to get more people to worship you?' asked Freya. Who did they think she was? A guru? A televangelist? She was just a schoolgirl. She had a vision of herself with a whip, lassoing people on

Oxford Street like runaway steers, forcing them into Fanes, corralling stragglers and pushing them inside.

'You must find a way,' said Thor. 'It's not your place to question us. It's your place to obey.'

'We DEMAND to be worshipped,' screeched Freyja. 'We are the Lords, your Gods. We created you from driftwood. We demand recompense.'

Freya cowered under the onslaught.

'But . . . you can't *make* people worship you,' said Freya.

'Oh yes we can,' said Woden. 'Just watch. I'll unleash such floods . . .' Then his shoulders slumped. 'In the good old days we would have smited you all for your neglect; sent tsunamis and hurricanes and pestilence but . . . we can't any more.'

'You want to *force* people to worship you?' asked Freya. '*Scare* people into worshipping you?'

'The ways of Gods are not to be understood by mortals,' said Thor.

'Frankly, we don't care *why* we're worshipped,' said the Goddess. 'But worshipped we must be. We all know what happens to Gods when people stop fearing them. They just fade away, fateless. Maybe a rustle in a bush somewhere, or a breeze.' Her lip curled.

Freya's mobile phone, which she'd left on the coffee table, lit up, with the ring tone of a barking dog. It was her father, calling from work in Dubai.

'It's alive!' the Goddess Freyja screamed.

Thor leapt up, raised his hammer and smashed the phone and the coffee table with one crashing blow. Then he picked up the flattened phone as if it were radioactive and hurled it across the room into a picture, shattering the frame. He dropped the hammer to the floor, breathing heavily. His red forehead beaded with sweat.

'No!' wailed Freya. 'My phone.'

'What is that thing?' hissed Woden, stepping back. 'How did you hide a dog inside it?'

'It's a phone, it lets you talk to people wherever they are,' said Freya. 'Look what you've done. The picture. And Mum's table. She'll kill me, what can I tell her?'

'The Hornblower can hear people at a distance,' said Woden. 'Like Heimdall. Can you hear the frost giants?'

'Not unless they have phones,' said Freya. 'What about *my* phone? It was my birthday present. What about Mum's table?'

'You see how much we need a guide,' said Woden. 'This new world bewilders us. To be restored to power we must understand it better. We need to study people, walk among them. We learn fast. You will guide us.'

There was a long moment of silence. Freya's mind was spinning. She felt dazed.

'No,' she said, shaking her head. 'You are definitely asking the wrong person. You must speak to the Queen or the Prime Minister. I can help you send a letter, maybe my mum can . . .'

'You alone can know our secret,' thundered Woden. He towered over her. 'You are the Hornblower. You are fated. You will do as your Gods command. We need to make people worship us again. We need to understand this strange new world and become like new Gods.'

Because the Gods commanded, did that mean she had to obey? She looked at him. Why is it always *me*? she thought. Can't someone else do the Gods' dirty work?

'Not me. Not this time,' she pleaded. 'I have to go to school, I—'

'We created you, and we can destroy you,' bellowed

Woden. 'Don't imagine that I am *totally* powerless. I can no longer send earthquakes or flood Midgard, but I can certainly bring destruction to one hearth.'

He looked around her sitting room.

'One charm from me and death and sickness will dwell here,' said Woden.

'Then who would help you?' asked Freya. She was taken aback by her own belligerence.

'If you don't, you and everyone in Midgard will die when the frost giants arrive,' said Woden. He looked at her fiercely. 'And since you murdered the giant Thjazi, you will be the first.'

Freya went rigid. 'But I didn't—'

'His death won't go unavenged.'

Freya's mind flashed to the giant's murderous claws, his hideous daughter, the fire and the blood.

'Skadi, icy with fury and burning for vengeance for her father's death, will join the frost giants on the rampage,' said Woden.

'Skadi?' squeaked Freya. She'd hoped no one would ever mention that revolting giantess again. 'Can't you *do* something? You're the Gods. I did it for you. You can't just let them kill . . .' Freya couldn't finish the sentence.

'You are not important,' said Woden. 'The giants are rising to re-conquer their ancient kingdom. They must be stopped. If you don't help us, the world ends . . . for us all.'

Freya hung her head.

Was there any way she could wriggle out of this?

'No,' said Woden. 'No one can defeat fate.'

Freya started gnawing on her sleeve, the familiar hollow fear in her stomach starting to squeeze her guts. How could one girl have made so many enemies? Speaking of which . . .

'Where is Loki?' whispered Freya. She didn't even like speaking his name out loud.

'Keeping well out of sight,' said Woden. 'Beware. When Loki makes an enemy he never forgets.'

Suddenly the Goddess let out a piercing scream. Freya jumped. Had Loki glared through the window? Was an iceberg ploughing down the road? Had the frost giants arrived?

'Look at me,' gasped the Goddess, rushing over to the gilt mirror hanging over the mantelpiece. 'I can *see* myself! What magic is this, I must have one of these, I—' Freyja's voice trailed off as she gazed in wonder at her reflection. 'I look a *mess*.

My hair! My face! My clothes!' she wailed. 'I bet I smell like a stray donkey. Tell your slaves to heat up the stones in the bathhouse immediately and fetch water.'

'We don't have a bathhouse,' said Freya. 'But—'

'How did I guess?' wailed the Golden One. 'What is this filthy place you've brought me to?' she snapped at Woden. 'I want to go back to Asgard and my lovely palace.'

'There won't *be* an Asgard to go back to unless we succeed here,' said Thor.

'I can run a bath for you if you like,' offered Freya. Anything to stop her whining.

'Run a bath?'

'Fill a tub with hot water,' said Freya. She wished she dared to just put in cold.

'An indoor hot spring,' said Freyja. She brightened. 'Well, go on then,' she added. 'I've never seen such shocking hospitality. I keep waiting for you to bring me hot water and a towel. What dreadful times you live in.'

Grimacing, Freya trudged upstairs to the bathroom and turned on the taps. The bathtub wasn't the cleanest, she was pleased to see. Should she put in some bubble bath? What the Hel, she thought, squeezing in a few squirts of Body Shop Jasmine. Not that Freyja deserved any.

She found a towel – why were all their towels so stiff and threadbare – and shouted down.

'Bath's ready.'

The Goddess flounced in and eyed the steamy white and grey tiled bathroom with the wood-panelled tub and the wallpaper peeling around the door.

'First good smell I've sniffed since I've been down here,' she said, inhaling the jasmine. 'Who will wash my back?'

'You're going to have to wash it yourself,' said Freya, and she walked out, shutting the bathroom door behind her.

She found Thor and Woden examining the television.

'What is this?' asked Woden.

'A television,' said Freya.

'Is it a weapon?' asked Thor, inspecting it gingerly. He lifted it up in one hand as easily as if it were a cardboard box. 'Do you hurl it at your enemies to crush them?'

'No,' said Freya. 'It's a . . . it's a magic box. Could you – could you put it down?' It was like looking after toddlers.

Thor dropped it. The TV thudded back onto its stand. Freya prayed it wasn't broken.

'What magic does it do?' asked Woden. 'I am the father of magic, and I am mystified.'

Freya grabbed the remote and switched on the television.

The Gods jumped as the TV thrummed into life and the sound radiated into the room. They stared at the screen. Thor cautiously crept over to peer behind it, as if someone noisy might be hiding there ready to leap out.

'Ooh, bad shot,' said the sports commentator.

'What magic is this?' gasped Thor. 'You are seeing people who are not here. Are they ghosts? Are their spirits trapped within this magic box?'

'No,' said Freya. 'It's just moving pictures of something happening somewhere else. It's called a TV. It's for fun. Watch.'

Click! Freya switched channels.

'Wot do you mean, the baby isn't mine? Then who's the father?'

Click!

'Fold in your egg whites very gently, or all the air will go out of them,' said the glamorous TV chef.

Click!

'You see, Inspector, I nearly went out of my mind after Bruce vanished.'

'So you too can peer into other worlds,' said Woden softly. 'Before only I could.'

'Everyone has a TV now,' said Freya.

'*Everyone?*' asked Woden. He looked pale.

'Well, yes,' nodded Freya. 'Almost everyone.'

'I can see anything I like from my High Seat Hlidskjalf,' said Woden. 'Does this magic box allow you this? Can you see the frost giants? Can you see the future?'

'No,' said Freya. 'It mostly shows you things which have already happened, or are happening now.'

Woden brightened. 'Ah, so some powers are still reserved for the Immortals,' he said.

Freya clicked off the TV.

'Look, I've been thinking . . . why don't you just tell people who you are?' said Freya. 'That you have returned? Everyone will flock to you again . . . job done.'

Woden looked at her.

'Weak as we are, the children of Heimdall won't believe us,' said Woden. 'We saw that on the bridge. Once we are powerful again, we will reveal ourselves at a time of our choosing.'

There was a loud banging on the front door.

Freya jumped as if it were Skadi herself come to kill her.

'Open it,' ordered Woden.

Freya obeyed, trembling.

Two familiar people stood there. One smiling. One scowling.

'Alfi,' breathed Freya. 'Roskva. Amaze-balls.'

'Is our master here yet?' asked Roskva.

Freya nodded. She was so surprised she could barely speak. How many more visitors would she be having?

Roskva was wearing a dress with a skirt over it and a pair of trousers beneath both. Nothing fitted quite right.

She scowled at Freya.

'Why do I have a bad feeling about this?' she said.

Alfi beamed.

'Freya! You made it home safely from Bifrost.

Sorry, that was a stupid thing to say, I'm just so glad to see you.'

He hugged her.

'Although probably not for long,' said Roskva. 'Not if Skadi and the giants . . .' Alfi kicked her.

'Ouch,' squealed Roskva. 'I'm just saying the truth.'

'What are you doing here?' asked Freya.

'We go where our master goes,' said Roskva. 'Where is Thor?'

Freya pointed to the sitting room. Then she ran to the kitchen and got out a packet of digestive biscuits. Should she serve them on a plate? In the packet? How did you entertain Gods in your home?

Back in the sitting room, Thor had stretched out and removed his gigantic leather boots. A dreadful stink of unwashed feet filled the room. Freya tried not to gag.

'Ooof, that's better,' said Thor, flexing his toes. He scooped up all the biscuits and swallowed them in one gulp. 'What do you call these things?'

'Biscuits,' said Freya. She glanced at the clock. Yikes. Clare would be home any minute. How could she get them to leave?

'I'll come and meet you tomorrow,' said Freya. 'Bring some ideas about getting you more worshippers. Where are you staying?'

'Here of course,' said Woden.

Oh Gods. Oh no. Not that, anything but that.

'You can't . . . my mother . . . how would I explain you?' asked Freya. She stopped as Woden's face darkened in fury.

'You dare to—'

A key turned in the front door lock.

It's Wodenic to Welcome Strangers

'Freya, I'm home,' came Clare's voice, as the door slammed.

'Don't tell her who you are,' hissed Freya.

'Gods are always recognised,' said Woden. 'If we choose to reveal—'

'Oh my Gods, how did the hall light break? Freya. Why haven't—'

Clare walked into the sitting room and stared at the dishevelled, oddly dressed strangers in their flowing cloaks and tunics crowding her small front room.

'Can I help you? Are you rehearsing a play or something?' Then she saw the coffee table. 'Freya, what's happened to my table?' wailed Clare. 'And Granny's chair. And my picture frame . . . Have we

58

been robbed? Are you okay? Freya, what's going on?'

'Uh, Mum, I don't know, the table must have been cracked, it just shattered when I . . . when I . . . sat on it,' said Freya.

'You *sat* on the table?' shrieked Clare. 'Or *jumped* on the table? It looks like it's been smashed. And I'm sorry,' she turned to the strangers, 'are you waiting for me? I don't normally see members of my Throng at my home without an appointment . . .' Her voice trailed off. 'I'm afraid I don't recognise you. Are you new Throngers?'

'The Hornblower's mother is my priestess,' muttered Woden to the others. 'Obviously doing a *terrible* job.'

'Sorry?' said Clare. She looked at Freya. 'Who *are* these people?'

'Mum, they're from Iceland. They're foreign exchange students and their teachers,' said Freya. She had no idea how that lie popped into her head.

Clare's face cleared. 'Oh.'

'This is Roskva and her brother Alfi, and their teachers. And . . . and I'm . . . we're . . . hosting them. Didn't you see the letter from Priest Ivar asking for volunteer families?'

She avoided looking at her mother. She was a terrible liar.

'What letter?' asked Clare.

'You know, the one I brought home.' How could Clare not see her sweaty hands?

'No I didn't,' said Clare. 'Freya, can I have a word?'

Freya, her heart sinking, followed her mum to the far end of the sitting room. Casually, she pushed her crushed phone under a bookshelf.

'You *volunteered* to host guests from abroad without asking me?' said Clare. Her voice rose sharply.

'Mum, keep your voice down, they'll hear you,' muttered Freya.

'You can't do this to me, when I'm so busy, and—'

'It's all right, Mum, I'll look after them,' said Freya. 'It's Wodenic to welcome strangers, isn't that right?'

'Need I remind you that the Traveller who has come from afar needs water, kindness, concern, and FOOD!' boomed Thor. He knitted his brows ominously.

Clare pursed her mouth. She sighed ungraciously. 'I am perfectly aware of the Sayings of the Gods, thank you, Mr – uh, what is your name?'

60

'Atli,' said Thor.

'Atli Bluetooth,' added Freya, saying the first surname she thought of. 'And this is—'

'Oski,' said Woden. 'Oski Bluetooth.'

'Those are fine, Wodenic names I haven't heard in a while,' said Clare. 'Are you two related?'

'He's my son,' said Woden.

'Really?' said Clare. 'I'd have said you were both the same age. Nice to share a profession, though.'

She peered more closely at her unwelcome visitors.

'What happened to you?' asked Clare. 'You look like you've been in the wars.'

'As a matter of fact,' began Woden, 'we—'

'They were mugged, Mum,' interrupted Freya.

'What a terrible introduction to Britain we've had,' said Roskva.

'But so much better since we've met you,' added Alfi politely. Freya beamed at him.

'Oh dear,' said Clare, smiling at Alfi. 'I am sorry.'

'It will greatly enhance your honour if you receive us,' said Woden.

'Really?' Clare looked doubtful. 'And how long is the exchange for?'

'Oh, just a few—' before Freya could finish speaking, the sound of splashing and loud, tuneless singing came from upstairs.

'Don't tell me there's *more*,' said Clare.

'That's Freyja,' said Freya. 'She's a—'

'All the brooch goddesses, glinting with gold . . .' brayed the shrill voice from inside the bathroom.

'How long has she been in there?' said Clare. 'Because I'd like to freshen up . . .'

'There's another magic glass in here,' shouted the bathing Goddess. 'I could admire myself all day. I want a hundred of these for my Hall.'

Freya looked at her mum and shrugged.

'They're foreigners,' she whispered. 'It's only for a few days.'

Clare marched up the stairs and knocked aggressively on the bathroom door.

'The Goddess of the Arm, the sea-fire's fortress—' came the trilling voice.

'Hello, could you hurry up please?' interrupted Clare. 'We only have one bathroom and other people need to use it.'

Freyja stopped singing.

'How *dare* you disturb me!' she screeched. 'Go wash outside.'

Clare looked stunned.

She opened her mouth, closed it, and clutched her brow. 'Freya, I really don't need house guests on top of everything else, especially not such *rude* ones . . . and there's a strange man lurking outside. He's wearing some kind of skins. And carrying weapons. I'm going to call the police.'

Freya peeked through the window. The unmistakable shape of Snot was visible standing outside her front wall, wearing bear skins and holding an axe in his club-like fist.

He raised his weapon to her. 'Hail and be lucky, Hornblower!' he shouted.

Freya started to feel faint.

Great. Just great. Three Gods, two slaves, and a berserker. Oh and frost giants on the way. Freya gave Snot a little wave.

'You *know* him?' asked Clare.

'He's their . . . umm . . . bodyguard,' said Freya. That, at least, was true.

'Bodyguard?' said Clare. 'Who *are* these people?'

'They're just simple Icelandic people,' said Freya.

If she told any more lies her nose was going to hit the wall. 'Not used to the big city. Their school wanted to send someone . . . in national dress . . . to protect them. And they were right, they've been mugged on their first day.'

'They're obviously going to need a lot of looking after,' said Clare. 'I mean, look at their clothes. And, so help me Frey and the all-powerful Gods, I just don't have the time. I've got baby namings, and a wedding, and an oath-swearing . . .'

'Mum, it's sorted, leave it to me,' said Freya, as the bathroom door opened, and the Goddess appeared, wearing one of Clare's best dresses and some of her jewellery.

Clare's mouth dropped open.

'Excuse me. That's my dress you're wearing,' said Clare.

Freyja scowled.

'And what a hideous rag it is, too,' said the Goddess of Plenty. 'You should be ashamed to offer a guest such a horrible garment.'

'I didn't offer it,' said Clare. 'You took it. And my shoes. How dare you just rummage in my closet and borrow my things. Those are my best sandals. And they're too small for you, you've stretched them.'

'You didn't offer me gifts when I arrived so I corrected your lack of hospitality,' said Freyja. 'It's an honour to have me as your guest, thrall.'

'You can't just take other people's things,' said Clare. 'Maybe where you're from that's okay, but it isn't here.'

'Mum!' hissed Freya. 'They do things differently in . . . Iceland. Her clothes were wrecked when she was mugged.'

'It's an honour for you to give me a garment,' said Freyja. 'But if you are so foolish as to require payment instead of my blessing, well then . . .'

Freyja stripped off one of her heavily carved gold bangles and handed it to Clare. Then she sashayed down the stairs in Clare's heels.

'I can't accept this,' said Clare.

'Mum, just take it,' said Freya. 'It's rude to refuse.'

Clare looked at the bangle. 'This seems awfully valuable,' she said.

'Cut them some slack, Mum, okay?' begged Freya. 'We want them to have a good impression of Britain, right?'

Clare sighed.

'And what did she call me? *Thrall?* What does she think I am?'

'It must mean something different in Icelandic,' said Freya. 'It probably means Enthralling Madame or Honoured Lady.'

Clare looked sceptical.

The TV blared from the sitting room, accompanied by loud stomps and cheers. Freya dashed downstairs. My Gods, you couldn't leave them alone for a moment, she thought.

The three Immortals sat riveted in front of the telly watching the Jewellery Channel as the blonde presenter modelled bracelets. Roskva and Alfi stood by the door, equally mesmerised.

'People offer treasure on this box,' said Woden.

'I want everything,' said Freyja.

'So you see what you get BEFORE you go raiding,' said Thor. 'Makes sense.'

'You can't just take things,' said Freya. 'You have to buy them.'

'Buy?' said Woden. 'That's just for merchants.'

'Where's dinner?' bellowed Thor. 'I'm starving! I could eat an ox.'

'What do you mean, where's dinner?' said Clare,

standing in the doorway.

'There should always be food for those who need it,' said Thor. 'And drink. Where's your beer vat? The good host always has one by the door for thirsty guests. And we're thirsty.'

Freya cringed. She rarely saw her Mum lost for words.

'I wasn't expecting guests tonight,' said Clare. 'I don't have much food in the house. We were just going to have a very simple supper.'

'You should always be ready to receive guests,' snapped the Goddess, rolling her eyes.

'The unwelcome guest is untimely,' muttered Clare.

Thor's hand twitched on his hammer.

'Mum!' hissed Freya. 'They're foreigners. That's the custom in Iceland. Please.'

'I want mead,' said Woden.

'A horn of shining ale!' bellowed Thor.

'I have lemonade,' said Clare. 'And ginger beer.'

The Gods looked unhappily at the soft drinks Clare served. Thor took a sip, and spat it out.

'Hope you've got herring. I love herring,' said Thor. 'And salmon. I can eat eight.'

'No,' said Clare. 'We *were* having fish fingers and jacket potatoes with cheese tonight. But I don't have enough—'

'What's a potato?' said Thor.

'You don't have potatoes in Iceland?' asked Clare.

Thor looked bewildered.

'It's a vegetable,' said Clare.

'That's not a worthy feast for guests like us,' said Woden. 'Why haven't you roasted oxen or a boar, or slaughtered a sheep?'

Clare's mouth dropped open. She shot Freya a look. Freya pretended not to notice.

'Freya, will you help me get supper ready?' said Clare.

Freya followed her into the kitchen. She felt like she was vainly trying to staunch a leaking dyke. Whenever one hole was plugged another opened.

'What abominable manners. Honestly,' said her mother. 'I've half a mind to walk out and leave them to fend for themselves. What am I going to feed them? There's not enough food in the house for so many, I could whip up some pasta, or macaroni cheese, but I don't have any—'

'What about pizza?' suggested Freya.

Clare's face cleared.

'Good idea. I'll order some takeaway. Are any of them vegetarian?'

Freya tried – and failed – to imagine vegetarian Gods.

'No,' she said, as Clare reached for her phone.

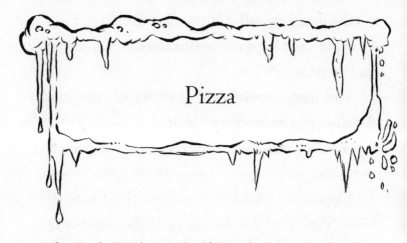

Pizza

The Gods, Roskva and Alfi squished into the kitchen, gazing cautiously at the crisps Clare offered. They stared at the stained wooden table in the centre, the result of too much finger-painting when Freya was little, with its bench on one side, and mis-matched chairs on the other. Freya hastily swept the papers and books off the table, to clear some space.

'*This* is your feasting hall?' said the Goddess.

'Yes,' said Clare. 'I'd call it a kitchen, though.'

'This hovel is very small and mean,' said the Goddess. 'I am used to *much* better. Where are the slaves who will serve us and fill our drinking horns?'

'If you will allow me to correct your English, I think you mean *servants*, not slaves,' said Clare, bristling. 'And there are no servants here, sorry.

It's the best I can offer at this *short* notice.'

'We ate and slept in the same room on our farm,' said Roskva.

'This house is *much* nicer than our old one,' said Alfi. 'No pigs indoors for a start.'

'Dad, look at this!' said Thor, pointing to the oven. 'And this!' he added, going to the refrigerator. He gasped. 'It's COLD in this box, yet warm in the room. And this!' He flicked the light switches on and off, on and off. 'This room is lit without fire or nuggets of gold. And this!' he shouted, pointing at the sink where water came from the tap. 'Water inside. I have 540 rooms in my Hall, and none have anything like this.'

'540 rooms?' said Clare. Mr Bluetooth must be confused about his numbers in English, she thought.

'You have light without candles,' said Woden. 'And water without a well. Yet this is far from being a great hall.'

Clare's brows furrowed.

'They live in a very rural part of Iceland, Mum,' said Freya.

Clare smiled patiently. 'You speak excellent English.'

'We speak many languages,' said Woden.

'Right everyone, sit down, sit anywhere,' said Clare. 'We'll all have to squeeze in.'

'I will take the High Seat,' said Woden, pushing past Clare and placing himself at the head of the table.

'Mr Bluetooth, why don't you sit next to your dad,' began Clare.

Thor's eyebrows bristled.

'You've seated me by the door,' he roared. 'I am insulted. I want a better seat.'

Clare jumped.

'I'll switch with him,' said Freya. 'He's nervous about doors,' she whispered. Oh Gods, what next?

Roskva and Alfi went and stood behind Thor's chair.

'Fine, fine,' said Clare, flustered, 'and Roskva and Alfi can sit . . .'

'On the floor,' said Thor.

'What?' asked Clare.

'Mum, students don't eat with teachers in Iceland,' said Freya.

'Well. I'm afraid they do in Britain,' said Clare firmly.

Thor scowled.

'We must follow the custom of the country,' said Woden. 'Bid the slaves sit at the far end of the table.'

'Slaves?' said Clare. 'I—'

'Mum, it's Icelandic for student,' interrupted Freya. 'It's pronounced *Slowe-ve*. We learned that today in school when we were hearing about the exchange students.'

Clare paused. 'I must remember that,' she said. 'Very interesting. I might use it in my sermon this week, how important it is to honour children, and not treat them as commodities.'

Roskva and Alfi seated themselves awkwardly. Freya looked at them. Help me out here, she begged silently.

'We are looking forward to seeing more of your beautiful town, Priestess,' said Alfi.

'Why not take a bus tour?' suggested Clare.

Freya looked gratefully at her mum. That was a wonderful idea.

'Bus?' said Thor.

'You know, big, red, double-decker,' said Clare.

'A chariot for many people,' said Freya.

'Pulled by goats?' asked Thor.

The doorbell rang.

Freya froze. Were yet more Gods coming to camp out with her?

Clare came back into the kitchen carrying four steaming cardboard boxes. Freya breathed again as Clare set the large pizzas out on platters and placed them in the centre of the crowded table.

'Food at last,' said Clare. Freya could see how tense she was.

The Goddess Freyja sighed loudly.

'About time,' she said. She held up a fork. 'What is this for? To stab enemies?'

'A fork,' said Clare. 'To eat with.'

The Goddess frowned. 'What's wrong with your fingers?'

'What is this strange food?' asked Woden.

'Pizza,' said Clare. 'I'll just slice—'

Thor scooped up the gargantuan chicken and pineapple pizza, shoved it whole in his mouth and gulped it down.

'Tasty,' he said, wiping his mouth. 'I'll have another ten.'

'Ten?' said Clare weakly.

'I'm hungry!' bellowed Thor, grabbing a second one and guzzling it whole. 'It's been a long day.'

The great God of Storms and Justice was such a pig, thought Freya. She avoided her mother's eye.

'Freya says you're all teachers,' said Clare, passing round the remaining slices away from Thor. Her hand shook slightly. 'So . . . what subjects do you teach? English?'

Woden smiled.

'Poetry. War. Magic,' he said.

'Like the All-Father,' said Clare. 'How interesting. Are you a professor of Wodenic studies?'

'You might say that,' said Woden.

'Justice and law,' said Thor.

'Fertility and sex—' said Freyja.

'She means sex education,' said Freya.

Clare picked up her sliver of pizza then put it down.

'What an incredible coincidence,' she said. 'You all teach the subjects that the Almighty Gods you were named for represent. Come to think of it, what a coincidence that your parents all named you after the All-powerful Gods. Like I did with Freya.'

Woden bristled.

'We are not *named* after the Gods, we *are* the—'

'—teachers,' said Freya.

'Gods,' said Woden.

Clare choked on a piece of crust.

'Excuse me?' said Clare.

'You're my priestess. You should recognise me,' said Woden angrily.

Clare looked at him.

'He means they are *Gods* to their students,' said Freya. 'Isn't that right, Roskva?'

'They are Gods to us all,' she agreed.

✳

After the longest dinner of her life, Freya suggested watching TV.

As the Gods sat riveted in front of the telly, squabbling over who controlled the remote and flicking madly between channels, Clare asked Freya to come up to her study. What now? Reluctantly, Freya followed Clare to her small office on the landing.

'Freya, I know this is arranged through your school, but those teachers don't seem quite *right* to me,' said Clare.

'Really?' said Freya. 'They're just . . . *foreign*. They have an odd sense of humour.'

'No, I get the feeling Oski really thinks he *is* Woden and not just named for him,' said Clare. 'It's not funny.'

'Mum, he is Woden,' said Freya. What the Hel.

'That's enough, young lady,' said Clare sharply. 'I'm putting up with your weird guests, I do not have to put up with your cheek.'

Well, she'd tried.

'Mum, never hold up to scorn or mockery a guest or a wanderer,' Freya quoted.

Clare flushed.

'I'm well aware of the wisdom of the All-Father, thank you very much, Freya,' she said. 'I am not mocking them. I am questioning their . . . sanity. That's quite different.'

'Mum, honestly. I bet they think *we're* the weirdos,' said Freya. That, at least, was true.

Clare opened her mouth and then closed it. Freya leapt at the chance to change the subject.

'Mum, I've been thinking, how can we get more people to come to Fane?'

Clare's face lit up.

'Ah, Freya, how lovely of you to take an interest,' she said. 'That's something I ask myself all the time.

Last Sunday we had a Throng of eleven people, including me and old Mrs Kelly, who dozed the entire time in the front row. I'm wondering if I should start tweeting, or maybe we should run a teen drop-in centre, or—'

'How about scaring people into coming?' said Freya. 'Warning them about the end of the world and how we need the Gods to protect us?' A note of hysteria crept into Freya's voice despite her efforts to keep control.

Clare stopped scrolling through her emails.

'Is something worrying you, Freya?' she asked.

No, thought Freya, just that frost giants are coming to kill me, and will freeze the earth while they're at it, and I've got three Gods camping at my house . . .

She smiled weakly at her mum.

'No,' she lied.

'Because you haven't been yourself all evening. Is it those foreign exchange people?' asked Clare.

'Looking after them is a big responsibility,' said Freya. 'That's why school gives us time off.' Wow. She'd just thought of that. She couldn't leave the Gods alone for a moment.

'Time off?' said Clare.

'Well, yes, to show them around London,' said Freya. 'They've already been to my school.'

'I'm sure your friends will be fine exploring London on their own,' said Clare firmly.

'I've been given the next week off, Mum,' said Freya. 'We're supposed to look after the foreign exchange students. It was all in the letter,' she added.

Clare sighed. 'Freya, there have been a few too many surprises this evening. And by the way, where's everyone going to sleep? If you'd given me proper warning I could have made arrangements.'

Oh Gods.

'Well, Freyja can sleep in my top bunk,' said Freya. 'Wo – I mean Oski,' she corrected herself quickly, 'can have the sofa, Atli can have the table, and Alfi and Roskva can sleep in sleeping bags on the floor of your office,' she finished. 'See Mum, it's okay.'

*

Freya lay in bed in the bottom bunk, and tried to ignore Thor's booming snores rumbling through the house. What a terrible day. What a horrible evening. She was so stressed she was sure she would never get to sleep.

The Goddess had refused to share a room, insisting she needed her own chamber, but had reluctantly agreed to let Freya keep her bed, so long as Freya would fetch anything the Goddess might require during the night. Rat poison, hopefully, thought Freya.

Then there'd been a bad moment when Thor had demanded that Roskva and Alfi sleep outside the kitchen in the hall, in case he needed them, and when Clare had protested, Freya had had to explain that students were very respectful of their teachers in Iceland. Okay, it was lame, but she was firefighting from moment to moment.

On the other hand, it could have been worse. Snot could have burst in. Thor could have bashed someone with his hammer. Woden could have started reciting poetry.

Luckily, Clare had believed her foreign exchange student story, and even though she wasn't happy about having so many house guests, Freya hoped her mum wouldn't make too much fuss. It was now Freya's job to get the Gods out of her house ASAP, and then leave Midgard with the roar of worshippers in their ears, powerful and ready to stop the frost giants before they invaded.

I think I got away with it tonight, thought Freya. Long may her luck hold.

But *how* could she restore faith in the Gods? Wodenism was dying in Britain. She needed a big plan to fill those empty pews.

But what?

Freya saw herself walking up and down Oxford Street with a megaphone, urging people to get to the Fanes and praise the Almighty Gods . . . or else. She'd seen people preaching on street corners, you could reach a lot of people on a busy street like that.

Meanwhile, she'd speak out at school. She would organise a club, tell everyone to go to Fane more, pray harder, bring more offerings, warn that the end of the world was coming soon. Her movement *Regain the Fane* would spread, linking school with school, Fane with Fane . . .

Gods willing, people would heed her warning and rush to worship. She saw her Mum beaming as she looked around her packed Fane, her ginormous Throng bowing and sacrificing and singing praises. How happy that would make Clare. To say nothing of the Gods. Maybe she could persuade them to perform a few miracles when their divine powers returned.

There was a sharp knock on her door.

'One more thing . . .' said Woden. He handed her a carved wooden box. 'If you value your life, keep this eski safe for us. Just in case the giants overrun Asgard, or Loki.'

Freya didn't need to ask what was inside. She took the precious eski, laden with the apples of youth, and hid it deep inside her wardrobe.

The God of the Bitten Apple

The red, open top, double-decker London tour bus pulled into view and stopped outside Green Park Tube, where Freya waited with the Immortals. Her heart was pounding. The Gods just charged into roads expecting everyone to stop for them. Snot had twice attacked a car.

Woden looked around, absorbing everything he saw, as if he were breathing in the new world, but Alfi and Roskva jumped with fright every time a bus went by. Snot bellowed and brandished his axe at anyone who didn't immediately get out of his way. Thor scooped up a basket of fruit from a street stall and guzzled the lot, ignoring the shouts of the market trader.

'The merchants here have so many wonderful

jewels,' babbled the Goddess, eyeing the shop windows. 'Even more than the dwarves.'

'The roaring chariots you have now,' marvelled Alfi, 'that move without horses or oxen or goats. And the palaces. So many great chieftains everywhere.'

'So many colours. So many people,' said Roskva. 'More in one place than I have ever seen.'

They bombarded Freya with questions.

'How can you think in all this noise?' asked Alfi.

'Or breathe this air?' said Roskva, grimacing and waving her chapped red hands.

'Why is no one armed?' said Snot. 'Are all the swords concealed? Bah! Soft times.'

Freya didn't reply. Walking with the Gods was like herding unruly children. Children with sharp teeth who were liable to run away or attack at any moment. She needed six pairs of eyes. For a wild moment she imagined herself strolling with toddler reins firmly harnessed to each God.

'Oy, wait your turn!' protested a tourist, as the Gods shoved to the front of the tour bus queue.

'Out of our way, driftwood. How dare you block us?' boomed Thor, pushing people aside.

'That's £20 per adult, £11 per child. Or get a

family pass for £50,' said the conductor, looking at them uncertainly.

'Pounds of what?' said Woden.

'You can't mean pounds of silver,' said Thor.

Freya blanched. She'd forgotten to bring money. Whenever she went out with adults they always paid. The Gods looked at her as if she could somehow magic that vast sum out of the air.

Snot reached inside his bear skin and handed Freya a crumpled wad of cash.

'Don't thank me,' he snarled.

Freya decided not to ask where the money had come from. She had horrible visions of Snot raiding houses and menacing passers-by, and quickly banished the image from her mind as she bought tickets.

Woden shook his head. 'People accept bits of paper instead of gold or silver. What madness is this?'

They climbed the slippery stairs of the open-air bus and headed for the seats at the front. They were already occupied.

Woden strode to the front row.

'Move,' he ordered.

The German tourists looked at each other.

'But vee vere sit here—'

'Move!' roared Woden, fixing them with his malevolent eye.

The couple scrambled to their feet and scampered to some empty seats at the back. Freya shivered. The air was crackling with cold as the pale, icy sun shone dimly through the clouds. The Gods seemed oblivious to the chill.

A woman approached the empty place next to Snot. Then she sniffed and moved away fast.

Snot smiled with his black, chipped teeth.

'Anyone sits next to me I'll kill them,' he muttered.

'We started all this,' said Woden as the bus headed slowly down Piccadilly towards Hyde Park Corner, gesturing at the stone buildings and hustle and bustle. 'We are greater Gods than even I knew.'

'Amaze-balls,' said Thor.

'Amaze-balls?' repeated Woden.

'That's what people in Midgard say now,' said Thor. 'I heard it on the magic box last night. We have to keep up with the times.'

'We do not,' said Woden. '*We* are eternal Gods.'

'If we're not careful, we will soon just be

worshipping one another,' said the Goddess Freyja, 'because no one else will care.'

'What chieftain lives in that great hall?' asked Woden, pointing across Green Park.

'Your descendant, Queen Elizabeth,' said Freya. 'The High Priestess-Queen of Britain.'

'Buckingham Palace has been the London home of Britain's monarchs for nearly two centuries,' said the recorded commentary. 'The Palace has 775 rooms, including over 200 bedrooms and 78 bathrooms.'

'*We* should be staying with the Queen,' muttered the Goddess. She held her dainty hands over her ears as an ambulance roared by, followed by two police cars. 'The noise,' she shuddered. 'Worse than a thousand clashing shields and clanging swords. The chariots belching smoke like chimneys on wheels. Horrible. The fires without flames. The painted images which keep changing. The stink of humans – Gah. I like the clothes though . . . not *yours*,' she added, wrinkling her face at Freya's leggings and jumper. 'And the *shoes*,' she added. 'I do like those clicky-clacky shoes. The heels on spikes! The sparkles! I've never seen anything like them.'

'They're called high heels,' said Freya. 'Hard to walk in, though.'

Freyja sniffed.

'I think I'd manage it,' she said.

'Give you bunions,' said Freya. 'That's what my mum says, anyway.'

'You must suffer for beauty,' said the flaxen-haired Goddess. 'And it's obvious to all that *you* aren't brave enough. I don't like these carriages,' she added, as the bus jolted to an abrupt stop outside Marble Arch, 'I much prefer my chariot drawn by cats. It's a lot more – *Who* is that God?' she gasped, swivelling and pointing to a huge advertising hoarding of a muscular, heavily tattooed man in his underwear. 'And where are his clothes? How can a God be so poorly clad?'

'That's David Beckham,' said Freya. 'He plays football. He's not a God.'

'So you have built a shrine to another human,' said Woden. His face darkened.

'Not exactly a shrine,' explained Freya. 'He's a celebrity. He's selling underwear.'

'Cele-bri-ty,' said Woden, as if he were tasting the word. 'Cel-e-brity. So that is a new cult in Midgard

'. . . the cult of *celebrity*. Humans worshipping other humans . . . instead of worshipping us.'

'Hmmm,' said the Goddess. She turned to Woden. 'After his next battle, we must send the Valkyries for him. I'd like to have him in Valhalla.' She smirked.

As the bus headed down Regent Street, Freya saw a huge queue waiting outside the massive arches of the Apple store. Despite the cold, several customers had set out chairs and laid out sleeping bags. Woden stiffened. Thor craned his neck as the bus went slowly past the packed shop, staring at the people crowding around the laptops inside, heads bent over the screens like devotees bowing before altars.

'What is that temple?' asked Thor.

'What God are those people waiting to honour?' asked Woden.

'That's the Apple store,' said Freya. 'They're queuing to be first to get a new computer.'

'That's no market place,' said Woden. 'That temple houses the God of the Bitten Apple.' He pointed to the white Apple logo. 'Don't lie. We can see the crowds flocking to his ice temple, bowing low and worshipping before his shining altars.'

'Apples are the symbol of *OUR* immortality,'

said Thor. 'How dare another God presume in this way.'

'The bitten apple insults us,' said Woden fiercely. Snot clenched his axe.

'They're not altars, they're computers,' said Freya. 'People are working, not worshipping.'

The Gods looked at one another.

How could she explain computers to them?

'A computer is . . . a tablet of wisdom,' said Freya. 'A seeress of numbers.'

Woden's eye flashed.

'I sacrificed my eye for wisdom,' he murmured. 'I hung on the windswept tree Yggdrasil for nine nights, stabbed with a spear, to gain secret knowledge and magic runes. And now you say that these tablets are available to . . . all?' He looked sick.

'Well, yes,' said Freya. 'Anyone who can afford to buy one.'

'Can these seeresses tell you how to make a dead man speak?' demanded Woden. 'Or see the future? Or tell men's fates? Can they take wisdom and strength from one person and give it to another, as I can with one charm?'

'No,' said Freya.

Woden smiled. 'Thank the Almighty Gods for that,' he said.

'Who are those people lying in the doorways of the great halls?' asked Alfi.

'They're homeless,' said Freya. 'They have nowhere else to go.' Her face brightened. 'Maybe Woden could help them.'

Woden turned away.

'The weak must fend for themselves,' he said. 'All have a chance to win wealth and glory. Those without luck, those who fail, do not concern us.'

'Oh,' said Freya. For a moment she felt bleak and wintry. She hoped she would not be one of the luckless ones, scorned by fate, and beneath the Gods' notice.

'We are now approaching Woden's Temple, which alone survived the Blitz in World War Two,' said the bus commentary. 'It was built in the English Baroque style by the famous architect Sir Kotter Wren in 4677. The 85-metre high dome is one of the largest in the world and has dominated the London skyline for centuries. The earlier Temple was destroyed in the great fire of 4666.'

'That's my Temple?' said Woden, craning to see

the tall domed building as the bus snaked its way towards All-Father Square. 'I approve.'

'A Temple dedicated to Woden has existed here for fourteen centuries, and services are held hourly,' continued the commentary.

Suddenly Woden stood up.

'Get off the chariot,' he ordered. 'I want to see my Temple and appear before my worshippers. We will go inside and witness the devotions.'

They got off the red tour bus and headed across All-Father Square to the wide entrance. Freya prayed that a bigger Throng would gather here than her mother managed to drum up in Holloway.

Woden frowned at the tents and banners spread out in front of his great Temple, filling the piazza in front. The Goddess Freyja held her dress tightly to her side, as if the protestors and campers might contaminate her.

'OCCUPY LONDON,' read Woden. 'BANKS GOT BAILED OUT, PEOPLE GOT LEFT OUT!'

'Who are these people desecrating my Temple?' he asked. Snot growled and gripped his axe.

'They're protesting against greedy bankers making themselves rich,' said Freya.

'Why?' said Woden. 'How did they get wealth? Farming? Trading? Fishing? Raiding?'

'Raiding,' said Freya. 'They stole our money.'

Woden's eye gleamed.

'So Vikings are called *bankers* now. Ha. Viking spirit lives on in *bankers*. Good for them. Are they keen raiders?'

'Yes,' said Freya.

'Glad to hear it,' said Woden. 'Smashing and grabbing, just like the old days.'

'But they've stolen from the rest of us,' said Freya. 'We had to bail them out, and they've kept the money.'

'So demand that your chieftains steal it back.'

'It's not so easy,' said Freya.

Woden snorted. 'You live in soft times. Hail bankers! Hail the strong!' His voice boomed around the square, as if magnified by a thousand megaphones.

'Hail bankers! Hail the strong!' roared Thor. A flock of startled pigeons hurtled skyward as the protestors stared.

'We must send the Valkyries for bankers when they die in battle against the Occupiers,' said Woden, racing up the wide steps and bounding into the hushed Temple.

Freya looked around the cavernous stone interior, milling with a few tourists, with the carved, red-timbered high altar at the far end covered with offerings of fruit, vegetables, trinkets and flowers. 'Offerings are like paying protection money to a sacred Mafia,' her dad liked to say when he wanted to annoy Clare in the dying days of their marriage. Above the altar was the famous Turner painting of Woden hanging on the World Tree Yggdrasil. Stained-glass windows depicting Woden raising the dead, Thor wrestling with the world-serpent, and Tyr sacrificing his hand to the wolf Fenrir, were blurry with dirt and let little light into the gloomy interior. Statues of Woden clutching his spear which never missed its target, accompanied by eagles and ravens, and the heroes of Valhalla performing valorous deeds of dragon-slaying and troll-felling ringed the side shrines, candles flickering before them.

Huge marble busts of Valkyries stood on either side of the high altar. The hushed damp smell of incense and wax hung over the rows of mostly empty wooden pews, decorated with unlocking fetters and runic inscriptions, the shuffling boy choir in their worn vestments, and the flowers already wilting from a recent baby-naming or wedding.

Woden scowled. 'This empty barn is my greatest temple?' he hissed. '*This* is where my raven-rites are performed?'

Freya nodded.

'Why isn't it full of worshippers like the Temple of the Bitten Apple?' he demanded, striding up the gloomy nave past marble statues of all the Immortals. 'What does that god have that I don't?'

Better advertising? thought Freya. Customer service? Phones?

The Goddess Freyja stopped before a marble statue showing her standing in her cat-drawn chariot.

'Is that ugly sow supposed to be me?' she shrieked. 'I'm much more beautiful than that.' Her jarring voice rang through the Temple.

Freya counted the Throng assembled in the small, roped-off area at the front, waiting for the service to start. Only seven, not including her and the Gods. It was just like Clare's Fane, with another old Mrs Kelly already sound asleep in the front row, her wispy iron-grey hair sticking out from under a beanie hat she probably never took off. There was one family who no doubt needed to prove regular Fane attendance in order to get their whiny child into the local Fane school. Freya saw that the dad had already hidden his mobile in his lap. Once they had the school place, they'd never come back.

'Hopefully more people will be along any minute,' Freya said as brightly as she could. 'Often there's a rush just before the services start.'

Woden surveyed the pitiful Throng.

'Where's today's sacrifice?' he said.

'We don't do sacrifices,' whispered Freya.

'What?' shouted Woden.

The old lady dozing in the front row woke up, turned round and glared at him.

'SHHHH!' she hissed.

'No sacrifices,' said Freya. 'That stopped ages ago.'

She shrank back as Woden's face turned purple and red with rage.

'Not even an ox?' said Woden.

'A goat?' said Thor.

'A chicken?' said Freyja.

Freya shook her head.

'What kind of worship is this?' asked Woden.

'No wonder we've lost our powers,' said Thor.

'What do you expect from such creatures?' said the Goddess.

'You created us,' said Freya.

Thor sniffed. 'What's on the oath ring?'

Freya looked at the large plaited silver ring kept on the high altar, reddened with wine from earlier oaths.

'Wine,' she said.

'Wine? *Wine?*' bellowed Thor.

'Shhh,' said Freya. 'You're not supposed to yell in here. It's red wine.'

'Not sacrificial blood? What kind of useless oath is that?' growled Thor.

The Priest, in his long white robes, appeared from a side door and stood before the Throng. He beckoned them to rise.

'We are gathered to give praise to Woden, the all-wise and all-powerful, who gives victory and riches and wisdom, according to his will, inspiration to poets, following winds to sailors. And we give thanks to all the Immortal Eternal Gods, mighty protectors, providers of bread and wine, for their many gifts.

'Praise is cheap,' muttered Woden. 'Where are the drowned slaves?'

'And what about Thor?' asked Thor.

'Restore us, oh Gods, let us find favour in your sight. You made us in your image—'

'I most certainly did not,' said Woden.

'Fate is stronger than everything, even stronger than the Gods,' intoned the Priest. 'This brief life is all we have; the world to come is reserved for our bravest warriors, and the righteous, and the poets, who will have their own place in Asgard, as our archpriests decreed. Be mindful of your reputation. Our shrouded Life is brief, but fame is forever.'

'So far, not *nearly* good enough,' hissed Woden.

'What is the purpose of life? The Gods teach us it is to worship them and to gain renown by brave deeds. While the Immortals cannot always keep us from danger, we give thanks for the blessing of courage to face whatever fate decrees and the chance to gain our place in Valhalla.

'Now, my assistant Priestess will get out her guitar, and let's all sing together, hymn 27 in your Eddas, "Woden loves us every one".

Woden loves us one and all;
Thor protects in stormy squall——'

'You call this heap of mare droppings worship?' said Woden loudly. 'This *mewling*? Where are the hanged men pierced with spears?'

'Where's my altar of sacred rocks?' grunted Thor.

'Where are the sacred groves?' asked Freyja.

'*Where* are all the worshippers?' shouted Woden.

'Shush!' hissed a middle-aged woman in a hat in front of him, singing loudly. 'Show some respect.'

'Let us now recite the Wodenic Creed together,' continued the Priest. Freya saw him catch the eye of the security guards at the exits.

The Throng chanted:

I believe in the All-Father, creator of heaven and earth; and in Thor his son, Frigg his wife, and Freyja, Frey, Njord, Heimdall, Baldr, Tyr, and the All-Mighty Immortals. I believe they alone are the true Gods. I believe that Tyr sacrificed his right hand to keep the world safe from the Wolf. I believe that Woden hung for nine nights on the sacred tree, Yggdrasil. Long may they reign over us, until the Wolf swallows the sun. Amen.

The organ struck up a solemn melody, and the Throng stood for the final prayers and hymns.

'Stop! This is a travesty! Call this worship?' bellowed Thor. He jumped up and stood on the pew, red-faced and furious. 'What an insult!' His voice boomed and echoed around the Temple, ringing out over the organ, which tried to drown him out with a vociferous cadenza. Woden leapt to his feet and strode down the aisle towards the priest. 'I am Woden! The All-Father! May you be people without luck! May you never enter Valhalla! The trolls take you all! Where are the sacrifices? Where are the offerings? Where are the two-day feasts? Call this caterwauling the worship of the Gods who made you? You ungrateful sacks of wood! You hags, you pisshorns! ON YOUR KNEES! WE ARE THE LORDS YOUR GODS!'

Freya shrank into her seat.

'I'm going to have to ask you all to leave now, sir,' said a Fane official.

'This is *my* Temple, how dare you ask me to leave?' said Woden. 'Don't you know who I am?'

'You're a very rude man,' shouted the old lady in the front.

'Disgraceful,' muttered another elderly lady.

'Come on, we should go,' hissed Freya. She was hot and embarrassed. If she'd had her falcon skin with her she'd have taken flight. How did he expect people to worship him if he called them pisshorns?

'Say the word, and I'll kill them all,' growled Snot.

'No!' said Freya. 'You won't help our cause by killing people in your temple.'

'Master, we should go,' said Alfi.

'You can punish these people later,' said Roskva.

The Gods stormed out of the temple, ranting.

'Those weren't worshippers,' said Woden. 'They were gawpers. Sightseers. Their paltry prayers were without fervour. I felt nothing. Nothing! Not an ounce of extra strength.'

'That's why,' said Freya, feeling more and more like a cheerleader rallying her dispirited team, 'we are going out right now to get worshippers. I know we can do this. Follow me.'

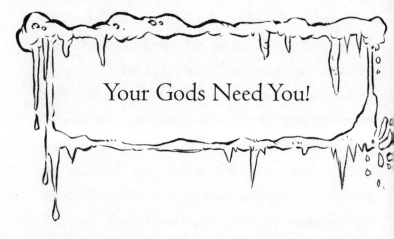

Your Gods Need You!

A few hours later Freya stood on Oxford Street outside the Bond Street Tube shops. The intense rain had turned into a thundery storm, flooding the street. The soaked Gods clustered under a jeweller's awning, where diamonds and sapphires twinkled behind thick glass. The jewels dispelled for a moment their grumpiness. Roskva and Alfi watched the milling crowds nervously. Snot stood with his right hand gripping the hilt of his concealed sword.

'I want that one,' said the Goddess, eyeing a heavy diamond and gold bracelet. She raised her arm to smash in the window.

'NO!' yelled Freya. 'You can't just snatch stuff here.'

'I want and I don't see why I shouldn't get,' said Freyja. 'What's the point of being a Goddess if you can't get what you want when you want it?'

'We can raid later,' said Woden. 'Keep your mind on our great task.'

The Goddess scowled, but said nothing.

Freya held a microphone, one of Clare's that she used for Fane socials and the annual square dance. She glanced at her uneasy companions, so strange and foreign-looking in their tunics and cloaks with brooches and gold armbands and flowing hair. 'Great costumes,' muttered one girl as she passed them, shoulders braced against the wind and rain, her umbrella blown inside out.

Well the Hari Krishnas looked even weirder in their orange robes prancing around with tambourines and chanting, thought Freya, so hopefully the Gods won't stick out too much. Just enough to make an impact.

'We tried announcing our return on the bridge, you know,' said Woden. 'And we got trampled for our pains.'

'Yes but this time we are urging people to worship you by telling them why they should,' said Freya.

'Trust me,' she added, with a confidence she didn't feel.

All six held cardboard placards. Freya had worked hard on her slogans before setting out. She'd considered 'The Gods love you,' but since they didn't, not really, she'd decided it would be better to write more truthful sayings, like 'The Gods give victory'; 'Pray to Woden and triumph over your enemies'; or 'Without Woden we're snowed in!' That was catchy – and true. But she needed to exhort people to action so she'd printed on hers: COME BACK TO THE GODS on the front and A PRAYER A DAY KEEPS THE FROST GIANTS AWAY on the back.

Thor carried THOR GIVES YOU MORE.

Woden had BE A WINNER WITH WODEN.

Freyja, looking sulky, held up LUCK AND LOVE WITH FREYJA.

Roskva's read PRAY TO FREY HE'LL SAVE THE DAY.

Alfi's said GODS ARE GREAT.

Snot's proclaimed WORSHIP WODEN OR I'LL KILL YOU.

Actually, that's what he'd wanted her to write

for him. Freya had written instead: 'Worship Woden – or else . . .' Snot stood scowling, brandishing his sign more like a spear than a placard. His gnarled skin, tree-bark arms and grey wolf's bristle would be enough to scare anyone off, thought Freya uneasily.

'Now what?' said Roskva.

'We walk up and down the street, and let all the people passing by see our messages,' said Freya. 'We also stop people and tell the truth about the frost giants.'

'And this is going to bring mortals back to us?' said Thor.

'Yes,' said Freya.

'How long do I have to stand here?' asked Thor. Rain dripped down his face and beard. 'This is worse than fighting any giant.'

'Good luck, everyone,' said Freya. 'Go up to as many people as possible and spread the word.'

The Goddess tossed her head and winked at a handsome young man sauntering by, chatting on his mobile. He stopped dead when the Goddess caught his eye. Soon he was joined by a cluster of men flocking round her.

'Hi, I'm Alfi, and I want to talk to you about the Gods,' said Alfi.

'Can I talk to you about the Gods?' said Roskva.

'No,' said a woman lugging heavy shopping bags.

'I need to talk to you about the Gods,' said Freya.

'Worship the Gods or I'll KILL you!' roared Snot.

No one stopped.

'The world will end unless we all start worshipping the gods NOW!' shouted Roskva into the microphone. 'Stop bartering, you trolls, and listen. The frost giants are coming!'

'Why aren't you worshipping the Gods, you conceited scum?' bellowed Thor, fixing people with his blazing eyes.

The shoppers bustled by as fast as possible and ducked into the Tube station.

'The Gods alone stand between us and the frost giants. Don't cast Woden's wise words to the winds,' yelled Alfi.

'The Gods, may their names live forever, have given us so many gifts,' shouted Freya. 'But in your strivings for wealth and fame, never forget Tyr, who gave his right hand to the Wolf for the greater good of all and saved us from certain destruction. We must all strive to be worthy of a God's sacrifice. Mighty Thor protects us. Glorious Frey and his sister Freyja give us prosperity. Woden gives us—'

Woden yanked the microphone from her.

'We created you from pieces of driftwood,' he boomed, his voice drowning out the din of traffic and hurrying feet. 'Then we gave you luck, to keep you hopeful when life gets tough *and* the chance to win the fame, which alone outlives death.' Woden's voice rose and his face reddened. 'So now it's your turn to thank us with your worship, you ungrateful herrings. If you don't, may fire play over your possessions and may it burn your backs!'

'I don't think cursing people is the right way to win them over,' said Freya.

'It's time to thank the Gods for all their gifts by worshipping them,' she shouted.

'The frost giants are coming and we need the Gods to protect us!' yelled Alfi.

I'm pretty good at this, thought Freya. She'd never realised how all those endless sermons she'd listened to over the years had sunk in.

'Cattle die, kinsmen die. The self must also die.

But glory never dies. Come back to the Gods!' she hollered into the crowd.

'I don't think anyone is listening,' said Roskva.

'Shut up and listen, you scum,' roared Thor, snatching up a passer-by and holding him in the air by his jacket, 'Or my hammer will shut your mouth. I'll hurl you all into Hel so no one will ever have to look at your ugly faces again!'

The man began to kick and scream. Thor dropped him suddenly, and he ran.

'May your end be horrible. May you never enter Valhalla,' shouted Thor after him.

Freya watched the crowds scurrying away from the furious Gods. A bus hurtled through a massive puddle in the flooded street, drenching them with water.

Slowly she lowered her sodden placard.

'I'm sorry, this isn't working,' said Freya.

Meanwhile

Buried deep inside a glacier, jagged and raw where chunks had crashed into the curdling sea, was the outline of an ice-locked giant.

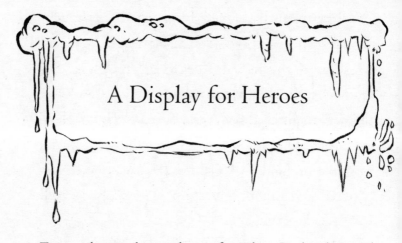

A Display for Heroes

Freya slumped on the sofa. The Gods slumped with her. Wet clothes steamed on every radiator and sodden boots and shoes lined the hallway. Clare, fortunately, was out at a Fane Council meeting, so wouldn't see everyone eating fish and chips on the sofa. They'd have to take some gold to a pawnbroker tomorrow, thought Freya, and get more cash, because they were eating Clare out of house and home. She'd given Freya several meaningful looks when she'd opened the fridge this morning and found it empty. She was already asking when the guests were leaving and when Freya would be returning to school.

Freya's legs ached from parading up and down Oxford Street. Her arms ached from holding up the placards. Her heart ached because her fate was so bad.

All her plans had failed. How the Gods thought shouting and shoving and sneering would get them worshipped she had no idea. The truth was, the Gods were much more appealing the less you knew them. Tears pricked her eyes. Her task was hopeless.

'I told you this was foolish, asking a mortal to guide us,' said the Goddess, picking a piece of battered cod out of her teeth. 'We might as well have asked a sardine.'

'Then what's your counsel?' snapped Woden. His grim face looked dark as flax.

The Goddess scowled at him.

'Return to Asgard and fight the frost giants,' said Freyja.

'Then we will all die,' said Woden. 'And a corpse is no use to anyone.'

Suddenly Woden shivered.

'The fabric of the worlds is tearing,' he said.

Everyone stopped talking. The Goddess went pale. Thor gripped his hammer.

Woden beckoned to Roskva and Alfi. 'Journey back to Asgard and look over the worlds from my High Seat,' he ordered. 'Return and tell me when the frost giants have broken free.'

Alfi and Roskva nodded and went upstairs to collect their things.

'They're *my* servants, you know,' said Thor. 'What am I supposed to do without them?'

Woden glared at him.

'We don't have time for this,' said Woden. 'The world is unravelling, and you talk to me about slaves?'

Thor glowered and clicked on the TV.

The thunderous noise of a screaming arena crowd poured out, as five floppy-haired boys danced and sang to a packed audience.

'You make my heart go boom boom boom!' sang the boy band, prancing around the stage in leather jackets and dark jeans. The crowd screamed and punched the air. Lights flashed and whirled across the stage, arcing and crossing above the singers and platinum-haired backing dancers twirling around them. An avalanche of squealing girls hurled themselves at the stage, hands outstretched to their idols.

'What is this horrible spectacle?' asked Woden. He peered at the screen. 'Are these berserks in some kind of battle frenzy?'

'It's called *FAME: Make Me a Star!*' said Freya. 'Those boys won last time.'

The Gods looked mesmerised. The audience was screaming so loudly it was almost impossible to hear the band.

'I don't remember a skald ever getting such a response to his poetry,' murmured Woden. 'No poets singing *my* praises were ever cheered so loudly.'

Thor looked like he wanted to hurl his hammer at the screen.

'They are worshipping those mortals,' he said. 'May they all be without luck,' he cursed.

That's it, thought Freya. That's it. She stood very still. We've been doing the wrong thing. Shouting on street corners? How could she have been so stupid? The Gods didn't need worshippers. They needed *fans*. Millions and millions and millions of *fans*. They needed to be adored. They needed to be worshipped as celebrity Gods. Once they'd regained their fame, the Gods would be strong and powerful again.

'I know what we need to do,' she said, trembling. 'We need to make you famous.'

'Yes,' said Woden. 'Yes. The Hornblower speaks wise words.'

'But we *are* famous,' said Thor. 'Who is more famous than the immortal Gods? Who exists who has not heard of my great deeds!' he thundered, eyes blazing, his red beard bristling, 'I drank the sea! I've slaughtered giants! I unleash storms! I need no more bright fame.'

'Yes, you do,' said Freya. 'If you want to be worshipped like the god Apple, and the god David, and the god Brad, and the goddess Angelina, and all the other new gods . . .'

'Do they defend the world against monsters?' said Thor.

'No, but—' said Freya.

'Do they fight giants?' he yelled. 'Do they give victory in battle? Can they calm the sea? Or blunt spears? Can they turn themselves into a fish or a snake or a bird? Can they make their battle enemies blind or deaf? When was the last time *they* raised the dead?'

'When was the last time *we* did, you stupid troll,' bellowed Woden. 'Without worship we can't do that any more either.'

'The new gods have no powers other than the ones their followers give them through their worship,' said Thor.

Woden stopped yelling.

'Exactly,' said Woden. '*That's* the power we need. The power we lack.'

'Yes,' said Freya. 'And as soon as you are idolised again, you can fight the frost giants. You'll be renewed. You'll be strong again. You'll be *Gods* again. But you need to be famous like people are famous now,' she added. 'Famous like – them.' She pointed to the sizzling screen. The Gods listened to the roars and cheers and wild applause as the floppy-haired boy band finished their next song, *Baby, you got what I want. Oh yeah.*

'You need to be celebrities,' said Freya. 'You said you wanted people screaming and shouting your name? Thinking about you all the time? Dying to know every little thing about you? Dying to meet you, to touch you, to connect to you, to know you. You want to be woven into our lives so we live and breathe you. You need to be in a TV show competition like *FAME.*'

'*Fame?* A display for heroes?' Thor beamed. 'At last you have told us something *sensible*,' he said. 'A contest where heroes and warriors compete for fame everlasting and immortality by doing brave deeds. Like our noble warriors in Valhalla. And the bravest is crowned and rewarded with fame for them and their descendants as is fitting. Yes.'

'Not . . . exactly,' said Freya.

'What do you mean, not exactly?' asked Woden.

'People compete for fame by . . . umm, singing. Or swimming or juggling or dancing with a dog, and—'

'And then they fight to the death and the bravest go to Valhalla,' boomed Thor. 'I'll make chopped herrings of them all. Let those fame-seekers beware. Alfi and I will—'

'No,' said Freya. '*Fame* isn't about fighting.'

'*Not* about fighting?' said Thor slowly. He shook his head. 'Then how can they do great deeds?'

'It's not about doing great deeds,' said Freya.

'I am lost again,' said Thor. 'Fame-seekers who *don't* do great deeds?'

'It's about performing,' said Freya.

Woden's grave face lightened. He smiled.

'Ah. Is this a fame contest for poets then, and not warriors? Where words are then reddened with blood? I am the God of Poetry and Inspiration, a song-smith like no other. No one can match me.'

The Goddess Freyja rolled her eyes. Thor scowled.

Freya shook her head.

'Let me see if I understand you,' said the All-Father. 'The fame-seekers recite poems about the Gods and our triumphs? Sing songs to honour kings and heroes and chieftains, to be rewarded with honour and bright gold?'

Freya winced.

'Not *exactly*, no. They sing songs, but—'

'You mean *we* need to find poets and skalds who will travel the world singing of our brave and noble deeds?' said the Goddess Freyja.

'I write poetry, if a poet is needed,' said Snot.

'We could bring Egil Skallagrimsson down from Asgard,' said Woden. 'His poetry always provokes cheers, and he could compose some new songs about our glory.'

'I'm already here,' said Snot. 'I wrote this today.' He stood and recited:

> *Oh Gods, foes of trollwomen*
> *plentiful of feast drink.*
> *Oh Woden! The war-god's wine pours forth*
> *Through my mouth.*

How the gold you give
glistens on your warriors' arms,
the grey eagle tears
at your enemies' blood wounds.

Woden beamed. Freya tried to imagine that song getting lots of audience votes.

'Not . . . umm . . . really the kind of songs they sing on *Fame*,' said Freya.

'But that is how poets and heroes eager for renown achieve lasting glory,' said Woden. 'The heroes do great deeds, and the poets celebrate them and give them immortality.'

'Not any more,' said Freya.

'If the songs are not about great deeds, then what are they about?' said Thor.

'Love, mostly,' said Freya. 'And bad boyfriends. About anything, really. Fireworks. Missing people. Being depressed and hating everyone. Getting dumped. Being beautiful inside when you're ugly outside. And then people vote on who they like the best. Can you dance? It's a bonus if you're a good dancer.'

Woden glared at her.

'I am the God of Battle and Wisdom. I am the God of Poetry and Inspiration and Magic. I don't *dance*,' said Woden. His voice was like ice.

'I kill giants,' roared Thor. 'I don't dance either.'

'*That's* how to become famous today?' said the Goddess. 'Singing and dancing like slaves? You're mad.'

'You dare to say that to have our Fanes filled with the children of Heimdall, to regain our fame and power, we must *sing* about . . . getting dumped . . . and *dance*?' said Woden.

'You can sing about something else,' said Freya. 'You know, form a band together . . . I could maybe—'

She stopped, seeing their furious faces.

'What's happened to fame for great deeds?' said Thor.

Freya shrugged. 'Times have changed.'

'So what you are saying,' said Woden, 'is that people without substance or bravery or skill or wisdom become famous.'

'Yes,' said Freya. 'That's the best bit: you don't have to be talented or special or even do anything. Today you can be famous for going to parties or for wearing nice clothes.'

The Gods looked stupefied.

'And for acting,' continued Freya. 'And singing. And playing football. And for marrying footballers. And . . . and . . . you can be famous for being on a reality TV show, or just famous for being famous.'

'To each his own way of earning fame,' said Thor, shaking his head.

Woden looked like he was trying to absorb a very complicated idea and not entirely succeeding.

'Fame should be earned and rare,' said Woden. 'Won through deeds which give immortality. How can it be, that *all* can be famous?'

'While we, who merit fame above all Gods and men, are desperate for reknown,' said the Goddess.

Wasn't everyone? thought Freya. She didn't know anyone who didn't want to be famous.

Gods damn it. I want to be famous, too, thought Freya. I actually deserve to be famous, after all I've done. I saved the Gods. I went on my own to Hel. And no one knows about it, except for some ungrateful deities and three friends who live in Asgard. It's so unfair.

'Have you quite finished, Hornblower?' said Woden. Oh Gods, she'd forgotten he could read her thoughts. What a shame *that* power hadn't vanished with the others.

'Everyone should be eager for fame and glory,' said Woden.

'Everyone is,' said Freya. 'We all want to be famous.'

'Who cares about them, how can *we* do this?' snapped the Goddess. 'How do *we* regain our bright fame? And how can *you* make this happen?'

Freya paused. How did someone become famous? It wasn't enough just to want it. How did fame happen to people? How did you get to that magic place where all your dreams came true?

They needed a fame-maker.

'We'll need help,' said Freya. 'We need a publicist . . . a fame-maker. But a publicist costs money. I don't have—'

Woden snorted.

He pulled a glowing gold armband off his wrist. 'Draupnir,' he said. 'Every ninth night another eight rings fall from it. Gold is not a problem.'

'Who do we summon?' asked Thor.

Freya's mind flashed to the publicists' cards buried in her shoebox.

'Wait here . . . I'll be right back.'

Freya ran upstairs to her bedroom and screamed.

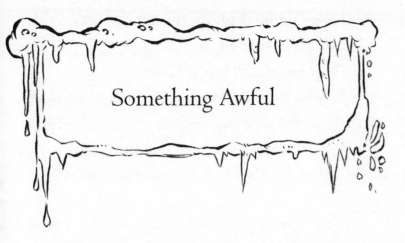

Something Awful

Clare was rummaging through Freya's drawers.

'Mum. What are you doing in my room? How dare you . . . snoop.'

Clare carried on searching as if Freya hadn't spoken.

'Mum. What are you doing in my room?' repeated Freya. 'I thought you were at a meeting. I didn't hear you come in.'

Clare shut one drawer and opened the bottom one.

What now? thought Freya. Mum's on the warpath. What had she done?

'Is everything okay?' said Freya in a small voice. 'If you're angry that I didn't empty the dishwasher, I was planning to do it after I finished my homework.'

'Who are these people, Freya?' said Clare. Her voice was cold and brittle.

Freya tensed.

'I told you, Mum, they're foreign exchange students and their teachers,' she said. 'Remember, I forgot to bring you the letter, and I am sorry, I—'

Clare looked at her. Freya suddenly realised that her mum was furious.

'I rang your school today and spoke to the head Priest,' said Clare, 'to find out how long I could expect these foreign guests in my house. And he told me something very interesting. He told me there were *no* foreign exchange students from Iceland named Roskva and Alfi. In fact, there were no foreign exchange students and teachers visiting the school *at all*. You've been lying and lying to me, and I want to know why.'

Freya's mind went blank. She opened her mouth and wondered what words would come out of it.

'Well? Who are this Roskva and Alfi?'

'Runaways,' said Freya.

'I see,' said Clare. 'And the beardy weirdy? And his evil-looking "Father" who looks younger than he does? And the Beauty Queen? Who are they?'

Freya stood there silently. She'd dreaded this moment. Why hadn't she thought of a clever answer?

'Are you in trouble?'

Freya opened her mouth to speak, and then closed it. She felt as if she'd been punched in the stomach, with no breath left.

'My Gods, Freya, what have you got yourself involved in?' said Clare. Her voice dropped. 'Who are these strange people?'

'Our Gods,' said Freya suddenly.

'Our Gods?' said Clare. 'What in Asgard do you mean?'

'I mean, Woden and Thor and Freyja.'

Clare stared at her as if she had just turned into a lizard.

'Freya, how could you be so gullible?' she wailed. 'No one has seen the Gods for millennia. What do they want, money? How could you let them into our home?' Clare was red with rage.

'They're not con-men, Mum,' said Freya. 'I promise. They're the ones I was with . . . before.'

Clare went white.

'Kidnappers?' she whispered. 'Right, I'm calling the police.'

'No!' squealed Freya. 'I had to help them.'

'I forbid you to see them ever again,' said Clare. 'They are out of this house immediately. And you will go straight back to school tomorrow. I'll phone your dad. For once he'll say the same thing.'

'Mum, you don't understand,' said Freya. 'I have to see them again. I have to look after them. My life depends on it. All our lives . . .'

'Don't be so ridiculous,' said Clare. 'Who are these people? Why do they have such a hold on you? Is this some kind of cult?'

Woden appeared. Had he silently walked in, or just materialised? Freya wasn't sure.

Clare blinked. She made the sign of the hammer.

'I don't know how you did that, and it's all very well playing tricks on an innocent schoolgirl,' she said. 'But I am Woden's priestess. You won't be tricking me.'

'Bow,' said Woden. 'Few mortals have gazed upon me.'

Clare stood very straight.

'Woden is a shape-shifter,' said Clare quietly. 'If you are Woden, prove it. Change shape.' Her voice rose.

'Mum,' said Freya urgently. 'Don't push him. Please.'

'I'm only asking, Freya. No harm in asking.'

'Oh yes there is,' said Freya.

Don't hurt her, she thought at Woden.

Woden glared at Clare. 'I am Woden, Lord of Victory. I do not need to give proof to mortals.'

Clare snorted. 'A very convenient excuse,' she said. 'Now pack your things and get out of here before I phone the police. I have worshipped Woden all my life. Don't you think I'd recognise him if I saw him? Just because you have one eye and call yourself by one of Woden's sacred names doesn't make you a God. Anyway, joke's over. I want you to leave my house. And keep away from my daughter.'

Woden's eye burned like red flames.

'Don't hurt her!' screamed Freya. 'You can't just smite everyone who disagrees with you.'

'I have met with better hospitality,' said Woden. 'You will regret your lack of welcome.' He stalked off.

'Freya, who are those people?' said Clare. 'I'm not asking again.'

Freya didn't answer. Behind her mother, on top of her chest of drawers, was the precious eski.

Freya blinked. She had definitely not left it there.

'Ah, you've noticed,' said Clare. 'Where did this box come from? It looks very valuable.' She reached inside and took out a golden apple. 'And why on earth are you hiding fruit in it? Please keep fresh food in the kitchen. It will go off and rot and smell and then we'll get mice and—'

'Mum, give me that,' interrupted Freya. Should she knock the apple out of her mother's hand? She walked towards her. 'Mum, put that back where you found it. Don't touch those apples.'

'It's just an apple, Freya, there are plenty more in the fridge. Unless those pigs have eaten them all. Honestly, what a fuss,' said Clare. Before Freya could stop her she took a bite.

'Mum, no!' screamed Freya.

'What's wrong with you, Freya?' said Clare, swallowing. Then her face softened. 'Oh my goodness, these are delicious, I've never tasted anything like this. Where did you get them?'

Freya watched, helpless, as Clare's body slimmed and firmed, her cheeks plumped and her hair gleamed. She dropped the apple on the floor, where it rolled under the desk.

'Ick, like what are these clothes I'm wearing?' shrieked Clare, wrinkling her pink cheeks and looking down in disgust at her midi-length flowery skirt, floppy cardigan, and low-heeled shoes. 'Like, hello, bag lady. Is this a joke? Did I forget it was Halloween? Am I going as a middle-aged frump?'

Clare looked at Freya as if she were an old crisp bag that had blown across her path.

'And who are you, anyway?'

'Mum, I'm Freya, something awful has happened, you just ate—'

'Mum?' said Clare. She looked around Freya's bedroom. 'Who are you calling *Mum*?'

'You,' said Freya.

'I don't know who you are, or what you're doing here, weirdo, but it's time for you to go home.'

'I *am* home,' said Freya. 'Mum, uh, Clare, something awful has happened to you.'

'How do you know my name?' said Clare. 'I've never seen you before in my life.'

'You have, Mum, you just can't remember because you ate one of Idunn's apples, and it's made you . . . younger.'

'I don't know any Idunn,' said Clare. 'Lame name.'

'Idunn? The Goddess of Youth?' said Freya. She faltered. 'You just ate one of her apples. By mistake.' Oh Gods.

'You know what? You're weird,' said Clare. 'And if you're one of those Gods-squad people, you can go away now.'

'I'm your daughter, listen to me,' said Freya. 'I think you should lie down.'

Clare snorted. 'Daughter. Ha ha ha. You're mental. I'm not exactly old enough to have a *daughter*, am I? And when I do have a kid, which I hope is never, she won't be an ugly ass thing like you. I'm going to change, and when I come back I want you out of my house. Geddit?'

'I'm not going anywhere,' said Freya. 'I live here.'

'I'm not a babysitter,' yelled Clare. 'Go home.'

'I am home,' said Freya.

'Fine. Whatever,' said the horrible mean teen Clare.

'Mum, why don't you lie down for a minute?'

'I'm going out and you can't stop me,' shouted Clare. 'As soon as I get out of these granny clothes. And stop calling me Mum, you freak.'

Clare flounced out. 'What are you looking at, weirdos?' she yelped.

Freya looked up to see Roskva and Alfi standing in the doorway, knapsacks in hand, staring after the raging Clare.

'Please don't tell them,' begged Freya.

Roskva pursed her mouth.

'We came to say goodbye,' said Alfi.

He looked at Freya. 'I didn't see anything. Roskva, did you?'

Roskva sighed. 'No,' she said. 'Keep your mother out of the Gods' sight,' she hissed. 'If they discover what has happened . . .' Roskva drew her hand across her throat.

Freya fought back tears as Alfi and Roskva left.

This was terrible. Freya thought she would faint if she didn't sit down. What would the Gods do to her when they discovered a bite had been taken from one of Idunn's apples? Freya shuddered. What would they do to Clare? When Alfi nibbled on a thigh bone from Thor's magic goat he and Roskva got enslaved for eternity.

There was a clomping down the hall and Clare reappeared. She'd squeezed herself into a pair of micro shorts Freya had outgrown, fishnet tights and a skimpy, tight red vest top. She'd added some black patent stilettos, and had slathered on a ton of make-up.

'Mum, you can't go out like that,' said Freya.

'Who are you to tell me what to wear? I'll wear what I want and you can't stop me,' shouted Clare. 'And stop calling me Mum.'

She stomped downstairs and slammed the front door as hard as she could. Freya prayed the Gods hadn't noticed. How long would it take before the effects of the apple wore off? *Would* they wear off? And how could she keep the Gods from ever seeing Clare again? She'd have to find some way of getting them to leave – fast.

The apple. Where was it? Freya got down on her hands and knees and scrabbled under her desk. She found the apple where it had rolled behind the bin. There was no bite – the apple had healed itself and become whole again. Quickly, she put the apple in the box and hid the eski back in her wardrobe.

I'd better call Dad, thought Freya. She took out her new phone and started dialling. Then she paused. To say what? 'Help. Mum's eaten one of Idunn's apples and it's turned her into the mean teen from Hel? Oh, and it's a bit crowded here, because three Gods and two slaves and a berserker have moved in.'

Freya clapped her hand to her mouth. Clare had been all set to lead evening services for the first day of harvest rituals. Somehow she didn't think teen Clare was heading to the Fane. More likely a club. Freya shuddered. Mum clubbing.

She speed-dialled the Fane. Mum's assistant priest, Karl, answered. 'It's Freya,' she said. 'Mum's not well. She's been told to take a break from her duties.'

That certainly wasn't a lie, thought Freya.

'Clare? Ill?' said Karl. 'I can't remember Clare *ever* being ill,' he added. 'What's wrong with her?'

'She's not herself,' said Freya. 'Can you lead the service for her? And take services for the next few days?'

'Is Clare all right?' asked Karl. 'Is she resting?'

'She'll be fine,' said Freya. 'No need to worry.'

Worry, thought Freya. *Worry.*

A sparrow flew in the door.

'Worry about what?' said Woden, changing back into his normal shape.

'I thought you couldn't shape-shift any more,' said Freya.

'I have enough believers left to do *this*,' said Woden. 'Not an eagle or a hawk. But I can occasionally manage a sparrow.'

'Why didn't you do that for Mum?' said Freya.

'I'm not a dancing animal. I don't have to prove anything,' said Woden.

Yes you do, thought Freya. You really do.

'Where is our fame-maker?' said Woden. 'We do not have time to linger.'

Freya grabbed her shoebox. Quickly she flicked through the small stack of PR cards.

There was one at the bottom, Veronica Hastings. On the back was a handwritten message in looping green ink she'd never noticed before:

One day you'll need me. When that day comes, call.

It felt like a sign.

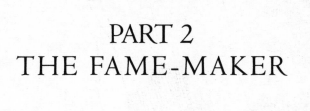

PART 2
THE FAME-MAKER

If you pursue your dreams with determination,
fearlessness and hope, anything is possible.

Britain's Got Talent 2011 Annual

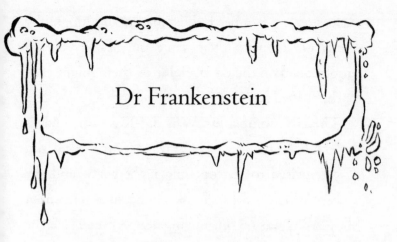

Dr Frankenstein

In her job, thought Veronica, gulping down the first of her many double espressos of the morning, you never knew what the new day would bring. Who would be up? Who would be down? Who would ring up in tears? Who would ring up and scream?

Clients were all the same. Absurdly shy and grateful at first, sure you were going to make them rich and famous forever. So thrilled with their first mention in *ICE* magazine. Then their first cover in *OH YEAH*. Then their first red-carpet appearance. First holiday in Barbados, every fab moment photographed for *FAME*. Modelling for *Vogue* if they were really fabulous – or *Glad Rags* if they were . . . less so. Singing a pop song if they could sing – or if they couldn't, it didn't actually seem to matter.

Releasing a perfume. Publishing an autobiography – any old tat with their name and *My Story So Far* emblazoned on the cover. Some of them might even bother to read it.

Then the complaints. Why did X get three pages in *WHIRLIGIG*, and he only got two? Why did Z get invited to the opening night party, and she didn't? What was his 'book' doing in a remainder shop? Why was no one buying her perfume? (Maybe because you both stink, she never said.)

Then the long slow decline to being a columnist for *TEPID*, calling bingo on a cruise ship, appearing on *Celebrity Makeover* and sharing your knitwear secrets with *CARDIGAN*, with the occasional yearly appearance in the gossip columns from Hel, '*Where are they now?*' '*When they were famous*' and '*Whatever happened to . . . ?*' And that's if they were lucky. The unluckier ones had their few moments of head-spinning fame then the plummet to oblivion, all in the space of a few short months. You'd catch a glimpse of them now and then, talking obstinately about a comeback, or the new album they were supposedly working on after being dumped by their record company, or their tummy tucks and new haircuts, and think, 'Whatever.'

Always new ones to feed the fame machine, she thought. The departure lounge was forever brimming with another hundred people longing to board the train to fame, fortune, freebies and fun. No matter how many times you warned them it wasn't forever, they never believed you.

Well. It was fun playing gods while it lasted. After all, she created her clients. Sometimes she felt like Dr Frankenstein, but not often. She turned the ordinary into the extraordinary – at least for a brief, fizzing moment. Her job was to promote average bundles of driftwood and turn them into gods: worshipped; admired; envied; idolised; magically endowed with divine powers of healing and creativity and generous sprinklings of fairy dust. She made legends. Everyone wanted to be famous these days, which was where she came in. Veronica the fame-maker. Pulling the wires from behind the curtain, making the scenery go up and down and the actors whizz on and off.

Veronica turned up the heating – heat! In September! Then she sat down at her desk, put on her orange lipstick, checked to see how much grey was showing at her temples – too much – and waited for the phones to ring while flicking through the morning papers to see which clients were pictured where. Phew, nothing about the unfortunate incident in the nightclub. And she'd need to speak to Lilith urgently about the way she allowed her nanny to always be seen taking care of her child while Lilith herself sashayed on ahead window-shopping. It looked bad, a mum who ignored her kid.

Her assistant, Thora, popped her head round. 'Your first appointment, Veronica,' she said. 'Freya Raven . . .' she dropped her voice, 'and a rather large entourage.'

'Her parents?' said Veronica.

Thora made her 'I dunno' face. 'And cousins and aunts and . . .'

Usually clients waited to see her *before* assembling an entourage, but in these fame-hungry days, you never knew.

'Send them in,' said Veronica.

This morning promised to be interesting. She'd been surprised to hear from Freya Raven last night, so many months after her mysterious return from gods-know-where, but if she was finally ready to talk, Veronica was sure there would be takers for her story. Obviously the price would be much less than before, since, quite honestly, people's attention had moved on. Still, there was a story here, Veronica was sure.

*

The girl peered shyly into her office. Veronica beckoned her in. She was followed by four people, a fierce hairy man who looked like a half-troll, and who appeared to be acting as a bodyguard (a *little* over the top; that couldn't be a *real* axe he was holding?) and three extremely tall, glowering, oddly dressed adults, all of whom looked like they'd come straight from one of those geeky 'let's all be Vikings for the weekend' role-playing games. Veronica grimaced. Oh Gods, here come the freaks, she thought. If this was Freya's family, no wonder she'd run away. Quite frankly, who wouldn't? They seemed even more awkward and ill-at-ease than the fame wannabes who usually cluttered up her office, and that was saying something.

Veronica peered at them as they towered above her immaculate desk, filling the office with their nervous, angry presence. Nervous she was familiar with. Anger was rarer. And intriguing. The tall man with the wide-brimmed blue hat had only one, glaring, eye, which was gross. Hello, eye-patch? thought Veronica, trying not to look directly at his empty socket as he loomed over her desk, fixing her with his cool, strange, multi-coloured eye. The other, red-bearded, man was huge, like a weight-lifter, and was for some reason lugging a decorated hammer fastened to his belt. Perhaps he was a builder on his way to work? An off-duty cage-fighter? A runner-up for Mr Muscle World? Whatever, it was pretty certain he hadn't showered this morning.

Standing with them was the most drop-dead gorgeous young woman Veronica had ever seen. Far too young to be Freya's mother. An older sister or cousin perhaps? A model? Actress? She'd slinked in, like a prowling golden cat, refusing even to look at Veronica, then she'd started fidgeting with the silver picture frames and looking like she'd pocket them if she could. Vain cow, thought Veronica, but then the beautiful ones usually were. She was used to being able to size up clients pretty fast, but these people eluded her.

Veronica arranged her botoxed face into a friendly smile and pretended not to notice when Hairy Half-

Troll sneezed into his hand and wiped it on his tunic.

'Freya, lovely to hear from you,' she said in her crisp, clipped voice. 'Sit down, sit down. Biscuit anyone?' she asked, proffering a plate of chocolate digestives. Muscle-Man scooped up the lot in one gigantic fist and stuffed them all in his mouth. His beard filled with crumbs.

Was she dealing with Oliver Twist here? thought Veronica, as she emptied the rest of the packet onto the plate and moved it fractionally away from Greedy Guts.

'So what can I do for you, Freya?' said Veronica. 'What's your story?'

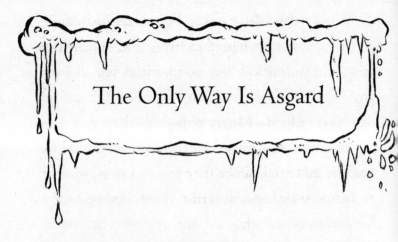

The Only Way Is Asgard

Freya gulped. They needed Veronica's help so badly. And despite the mint-green trainers (and spare pair of sky-high silver stilettos parked under her desk) and the spiky ash-blonde hair and the bright orange lipstick and funky dangly earrings, Veronica looked like a very scary businesswoman. Freya glanced around the office walls, festooned with photographs of Veronica with some of her famous clients, and took a deep breath.

What do I have to lose? thought Freya. The frost giants are coming. The end of the world is approaching. I can risk sounding ridiculous.

'I'm not here for me, actually,' said Freya. 'I'm here for them,' she said, gesturing at the Gods. 'They need to be famous again fast. They need a comeback. They need—'

'Whoa, whoa, let me stop you there, first of all, to have a *comeback* you need to have *arrived* somewhere first,' said Veronica. 'I have no idea who any of them are.'

Freyja flushed an angry red.

'To think we have to tell the driftwood who we are,' she muttered. 'Once they just had to glimpse us to fall on their knees in terror. It's so undignified.'

Woden grimaced.

'A bad beginning,' he muttered, looking dejected. 'That you even have to ask . . .'

Veronica pushed back her chair. 'Perhaps—'

'Are you a Wodenist?' said Freya.

Veronica looked astonished.

'Well *obviously* I was brought up as a Wodenist, but I can't say I'm much of a believer now,' she said. 'I'm in the hatch/match/dispatch group. Why do you ask?'

'Because *this* is Woden. The All-Father,' she added, in case Veronica might confuse this Woden with another Woden of her acquaintance. 'That's Thor. The Storm-God. This is Freyja. Goddess of Plenty. And . . . other stuff. That's Snot. He . . . uhh—' Freya didn't dare meet Veronica's eyes as she spoke.

'Snot is . . . a berserker in Woden's Valhalla army.'

None of the Gods nodded as Freya introduced them. They stood stiffly, raging. It was like having to introduce the Queen to someone who doesn't recognise her and doesn't want to know, thought Freya. She forced herself to continue. 'They're the Gods. Our immortal Gods,' she gabbled. 'They need to get their worshippers back, because without them they don't have their powers. And without their divine powers, they can't protect us from the frost giants. Who are coming, by the way.' As she spoke, Freya could hear that she sounded like a total nutter. Now she'll think I'm mad, thought Freya. *I'd* think I was mad.

'They need to get famous again. Fast. To be loved and worshipped again. All our lives depend on it.'

Freya looked up from her shoes and peeked at Veronica. Her heavily made-up face was impassive. She opened her mouth, and then closed it. A fly buzzed angrily at the window. *How did she keep those windows so clean*, she wondered. The ones at home always looked so grimy. Freya shook her head to focus her thoughts on willing Veronica not to burst out laughing or call security.

The silence in the room felt like it would last until the Wolf swallowed the sun. The Goddess sighed loudly. Thor fiddled with his hammer.

'Do you want us to go?' said Freya.

Veronica steepled her manicured fingers, then tugged on her hair. To Freya's surprise, she suddenly smiled broadly.

'Well, that's a bit different,' said Veronica. 'Makes a nice change from the usual client come to sell a story about her dates with some married footballer.' She paused for a long moment. 'Just thinking out loud here,' she added. 'So you're Gods, and you've lost your super-powers, huh,' she clucked sympathetically. 'That's a bummer. That must be tough. You're top dog, and then suddenly you're not.

'You've still got name recognition, which is a *big* help, so no need to build you up from scratch. But your brand is old and tired. Let's face it, you've been around, like, forever, and it's still the same old, same old. I mean, look at you, Woden. That hat! That cloak!'

'What's wrong with my hat and cloak?' said Woden. He bristled. 'That's how I am recognised.'

'Yeah, before maybe, but this is *now*,' said Veronica.

'Fashion is seasonal. You can't just keep one look, you'll bore everyone to death.' She stood up and started pacing behind her desk. 'We'd need to jazz you up, make you relevant, help you reconnect to the public, get those Fanes packed and the sacrificial fires burning, so to speak.'

'So you'll help them?' squeaked Freya.

'Sure,' said Veronica.

She took all her clients at face value. I'm a star-maker, Veronica thought. And a star-breaker, she didn't add. If these people, or Gods, or whatever, wanted to be famous, and had the money to pay for her services, why not? Why the Hel not?

'I'm not cheap,' she said. 'In fact, it will cost you £30,000 down plus £2,000 a week.' She glanced up to see how they took this. Money always shook down the no-hopers and the practical jokers from the fame tree.

Woden took off a glowing gold armband and held it up. Eight more heavy gold bands dropped from it and clinked into his hand in a golden waterfall. He spun them over to Veronica.

She picked one up and her manicured hand quivered under the unexpected weight.

'O-kay, that's a nice touch,' she beamed. She'd get her jeweller to make sure the gold was genuine later. 'Unorthodox, but I like your style, Wo . . . may I call you Woden?'

'I have many names, and that one will do as well as any other,' said Woden.

'Let's consider your situation,' said Veronica. 'Gods want to be worshipped. We want to worship Gods. The only question is, *which* Gods? You could say, who gets our vote?'

'What do you mean, *which* Gods?' said Woden. He glared at her. '*We* are your Gods.'

'Yes, yes,' said Veronica. 'Of course. Believe me, I'm at my local Fane most Sundays. Home-baked cakes made by my PA for you every February Feast Day. And Harvest festival. I never pass one of your altars without leaving an offering. Remember that lovely fruit basket? And the spring veg? That was from me.'

Whatever happened to her being a hatch/match/dispatch sort of Wodenist, thought Freya.

'I hate vegetables,' snapped the Goddess. 'Can we get back to how you're going to make us mighty again?'

Veronica smiled at her new clients.

'Look, you're popular. Sort of. Well, all right. Just not as much. In fact, not much at all to be honest. You've been away a long time and once you vanish from the public eye, other gods step up to take your place. If you snooze, you lose.'

'We were NOT snoozing!' hissed Thor. 'We were dying.'

'So long as WE are worshipped with fervour, and our rites observed,' said Woden, 'the false gods are of no importance.'

'Just so long as we're number one,' said Thor.

'Obviously,' added Freyja.

'Of course,' said Veronica. 'I only deal with the A-list.' All right, she had a small number of D-list celebs temporarily on her books, but they were the cannon fodder which constantly needed renewing after they had their 15-minute flight of fame and then crashed charred back to earth, to watch their identikit replacements take wing for their equally brief moment in the limelight.

Veronica looked at the Gods appraisingly. 'I'll be honest. You aren't in the *best* shape,' she said. 'Woden's only got one eye. Thor needs a haircut and a trainer badly. You all need your teeth fixed and whitened.

And Freyja, a *little* too heavy round the hips if we're going to promote you as a new *It* girl supermodel.'

'My body is perfect,' said Freyja.

I'll sort her out later, thought Veronica. A few rejections from model agencies and she'll be dieting sharpish. She pushed her frozen face into a smile again.

'So, reputation. Once we've reintroduced you to the world I can get the media on your side, polish up your image, and we can hush up any old skeletons in the cupboard – let's face it, everyone's got something they'd rather not have splashed all over people's cornflakes.'

Freyja's hand went to her necklace.

Thor furrowed his brow. 'Cornflakes?'

'A breakfast food for weaklings,' said Woden.

The phone rang.

'Hold my calls,' yelled Veronica.

'And obviously you all need new clothes. We'll get in a stylist immediately. No one will take you seriously in those old-fashioned robes and tunics. You look like something off the farm.'

'We have not changed our style of dress for millennia,' said Thor. 'We are Gods, we are eternal.'

'Well, that may go down well in Asgard, but here in Midgard we like our celebrities to keep up with fashion. And the tunic and boot look went out with the Vikings. You need to look contemporary, you need to look *with it*.

'Download Woden. Access Thor. Yeah, I like that,' said Veronica, mostly to herself. 'We'll set up a Facebook page for you ASAP. You need a Gods app,' she added. '*The only way is Asgard. Gods ahoy. Toga Titans.* I'm just thinking out loud here,' she muttered. 'The other problem is, I'll be honest, none of you look like Gods.' She thought of all the paintings of the glorious Gods in the National Gallery, the gorgeous, heroic deities striding majestically around their sparkling palaces, full of mighty power. Not this ramshackle trio standing before her.

'But we *are* Gods,' snapped Freyja.

'But you don't *look* like Gods, which is what matters,' said Veronica. 'Your styling is terrible. I mean, really, honey, that way too bling necklace? Pl-eeeze. Thor, that cloak is *very* last century. And Woden, that hat needs an update . . . maybe a baseball cap would make you more accessible.'

Woden grabbed his blue, wide-brimmed hat as if

he feared that Veronica was going to yank it off his head. Suddenly he filled the office with his presence.

'I am the All-Father,' hissed Woden. 'I do not wish to be . . . accessible. Without mystery, what am I?'

'No, no, I get your point, yes absolutely,' said Veronica, shrinking back a little into her swivel chair. 'But you're gonna have to trust me here if you're hungry for fame.'

There was a long pause. Veronica felt for a moment like an eagle was sizing her up for a snack.

'We're hungry,' said Woden.

'Then you'll have to listen to me and do as I say,' said Veronica.

Freya saw the Gods bristle. Veronica is lucky she hasn't been turned into a boar or something, thought Freya.

'Advice given by others is often ill-counsel,' muttered Thor.

'Do you want to be famous again, or don't you?' said Veronica. 'Because if you don't there are plenty of others who do. It's up to you. You have to really, really want it.'

The Gods murmured. Then Woden nodded.

'We do.'

'Okay. Once you're famous again, you start promoting the Gods. Where you lead, your fans will follow. We'll have you top of the pops and on the covers of *FAME* and *ICE* and *HURLYBURLY* and *OH YEAH* and *WHIRLIGIG* in no time. Plus you'll need to tweet.'

'Tweet?' said Woden.

'Talk to your fans. You know, tell them what you had for breakfast, your thoughts on the events of the day, a bit of Asgard gossip.'

'I do not eat, I keep my own counsel, and—' began Woden.

'We do not talk to men!' bellowed Thor. 'We are Gods. We proclaim, they obey, and that's how it is. We created them.'

'*I* created people,' said Woden, glaring at Thor.

'They need to get their fame back fast,' said Freya. 'It's really important. All our lives are at stake,' she repeated.

Yeah yeah, thought Veronica.

'Then we need to get at least one of you on *FAME: Make Me a Star*,' said Veronica. 'That's the quickest way to go from zero to hero. Fast fame is what I do best.'

Gimme everything, look at me, worship me, love me, fame. Keeping it is another matter, she didn't add.

'So,' said Veronica, 'any of you got any talents?'

'Talents?' said Woden.

'You know, can you do anything special?'

Woden looked, thought Freya, as if Veronica was a piece of rotting herring he had just stepped on.

'I wave my spear, and people die,' said Woden. 'I can raise the dead. I can see into—'

'Umm, I don't think dead raising would go down too well on *Make Me a Star*,' interrupted Veronica hastily. 'Death not a big winner either. What else?'

'I defend this ungrateful world against giants and monsters,' said Thor.

Veronica frowned. 'A little abstract, not sure we can import a monster for you to slaughter. Perhaps a bit too bloody for family viewing.'

'I can eat and drink more than any person living,' boomed Thor.

Veronica considered this. 'Speed eating is more of an American thing,' she said. 'Let's hold that in reserve. Plus I'm not sure you'd be worshipped for that, except by food manufacturers.'

'You can wrestle, Lord,' said Freya. 'No human

could touch you for strength, even now. And you're fast.'

Veronica appraised Thor carefully. 'Hmmm. I have a little idea about what we can do with you . . .'

'*I* can make anyone I choose fall in love with me,' said Freyja.

Veronica looked rapt. 'Wow, just think if you could market that,' she said. 'Love potions that *really* worked. Oh wow, I'd sign up in a sec.'

The Goddess surveyed Veronica with her cat's eyes and tossed her golden curls.

'I said I could make anyone fall in love with *me*,' she sniffed.

'Unfortunately, that won't make you too popular with women,' said Veronica. 'And we want to make you famous and worshipped by everyone again, right?'

Freyja stamped her foot. The floor shook as if a herd of buffalo had just rampaged across. Veronica jumped.

'If you only knew how *bored* I am,' said Freyja. 'How much I *hate* it here.'

What a spoilt brat, thought Freya.

'Thank you for sharing,' said Veronica. Honestly,

what she had to put up with from her clients. 'We might be able to do something with you as a model,' she said. 'But you'll need to work on your attitude.' And your fat hips, she didn't say.

Ha, thought Freya. The Goddess scowled and eyed Veronica's silver stilettos.

'I can recite poetry, the greatest imaginable,' said Woden. 'With words I can weave my own fame.'

Veronica wrinkled her nose.

'*Poetry?* I don't think so. We want you to win *Make Me a Star*, not be the designated weirdo loser. How about . . . dancing with a dog? Or drumming? Or magic? That's always popular. Maybe a novelty act with you in spangles, singing and juggling. We'll come up with a signature move, making a "W" over your head sort of thing.'

Freya saw Woden stiffen. His face darkened.

'I am Woden!' he bellowed. 'I created this world. I am not dancing. Or performing with a dog. Anyway, I hate dogs. I want to be worshipped, not laughed at.'

'Okay, okay,' said Veronica. 'Let's try the poetry angle. Maybe something modern, something rappy . . . it could work – we'll sort it.'

The Gods looked at one another.

159

'What implacable fate ordains must come to pass,' said Woden. 'The time for blood-wet spears will soon be upon us. We must be strong.'

'Won't they have to audition?' asked Freya. Somehow she couldn't see the Gods standing in long queues for hours waiting for their moment before the judges.

Veronica laughed. 'Don't be ridiculous, auditions are for plebs. I can get you straight on the programme.'

She picked up her mobile. 'I'll just ring the producer.'

Freya listened as Veronica chatted merrily on the phone. The Goddess stood, stretched, and then knelt down casually as if she'd dropped something. Freya caught a glimpse of silver tucked inside her tunic. It was the flash of a woman's stiletto heel.

Freyja had pinched Veronica's shoes from under her desk.

'What?' said the Goddess, seeing Freya looking wide-eyed at her.

'Nothing,' said Freya.

'Right, all sorted,' said Veronica, clicking her phone off.

'When do we tell the world that, you know,

Woden and Thor and Freyja *are* Woden and Thor and Freyja?' said Freya.

Veronica flapped her hands. 'First let's restore their fame. No point in leaking everything at once, gotta build them back up first. Save that for a big news flash later when the time is right.'

'Okay,' said Freya.

This job was going to be tough enough without babysitting a kid, thought Veronica. She smiled at Freya.

'Well, thank you, Freya, for passing your friends on to me,' she said. 'I can handle things for our future superstars from here. Off you go.'

Freya beamed.

Oh yes, she thought. No more lies and skipping school and having eyes in the back of her head in case the Gods did something awful. Why hadn't she called Veronica sooner? She'd been an idiot to think she could manage by herself.

She grabbed her coat. Wouldn't it be great just to do her history homework in front of the telly and ring Emily to find out all the gossip she'd missed? Just to be ordinary for a while, and try to forget about rampaging frost giants and fretful Gods.

That is, as ordinary as someone whose mum had just morphed into . . . Freya stopped herself from completing her thought just in time.

'Where do you think you're going?' asked Woden.

'Home,' said Freya. 'You don't need me any more.'

'We go nowhere and do nothing without the Hornblower,' said Woden.

Freya's shoulders slumped.

'I'm sorry?' said Veronica.

'Freya stays with us,' said Woden.

Veronica looked at Freya carefully. Why should the Gods care about such an ordinary schoolgirl? Was there more to her than met the eye? Nah, she thought.

'You must really like her,' she said brightly.

Freya grimaced. They didn't like her. They just wanted to use her until they'd finished with her.

'We'll need a consent form from her parent or guardian,' said Veronica.

Woden waved his hand. 'We are her guardians. Now swear a ring-oath that you will do all that you have sworn to make us famous again,' he said.

The edge in his gravelly voice made Veronica's skin prickle.

'Is that really necessary?' she asked.

Woden held out his hand, with its heavily carved thick gold ring.

'Swear.'

Veronica hadn't sworn a ring-oath in years. What I do for my clients, she thought, as she placed her hand on the ring.

'I swear by the rivers that run through the Underworld,' she intoned. 'May terrible fate-bonds attach to me if I tear this oath. Wretched is the pledge-criminal.'

The Gods nodded.

'Now can I make a few more calls?' said Veronica. 'You did say you were in a rush. Then we'll find somewhere suitable for you all to stay. I'm thinking the Ritz. Let's start as we mean to continue.'

The Gods looked at Freya.

'The Ritz?' said Thor.

'The Ritz *hotel*?' said Freya. 'Wow.' Her heart leapt. They'd be out of her house. Out of Clare's sight.

Was good luck finally on her side?

'Is that a palace?' asked the Goddess eagerly.

'As good as,' said Veronica.

She considered the strange people in her office,

and the fierce girl who seemed both captain and captive. Were they *really* the Gods, down on their luck and hoping for a comeback? Here in Midgard to reconnect with their fans — whoops, worshippers, she corrected herself. Or were they just crazy wannabes?

Veronica didn't know. Or care, really. They were interesting, they were different, and most important they could pay handsomely for her services. Either way, she was a winner.

Meanwhile

Slowly, slowly, centimetre by centimetre, from the deepest blue depths of the ice, sea-grey bodies clawed their way up to the splintering surface. The melting ice sheets heaved and buckled, crackling and growling, as crevasses opened up across the frozen plains stretching beyond the great cliffs.

Let's Party

The sound of blasting music hit Freya as she walked down her road. She'd sneak into her house, grab a few things and the precious eski, and move to the Ritz with the Gods.

Meanwhile, she was worried about her mother, though there was every chance the apple had worn off. She'd only taken one bite after all. Freya prayed she'd find one of Clare's bossy notes on the kitchen table, with instructions for dinner, then she'd leave one in return telling her mum . . . she was moving to the Ritz?

I must be losing my mind, thought Freya. Mum would never, ever agree. I'll just have to tell another lie, she thought. What's one more after so many?

My Gods, who could be having such a noisy party, she wondered. Clare would be straight on the phone to the council the moment she got home from work.

Then Freya realised the noise was coming from her house.

Cautiously, Freya opened the front door. There were teenagers everywhere, some dancing and drinking beer, others laughing and shouting. Several sleeping bodies were curled up on the sitting room floor. There were bottles and shattered glass all over the place, along with plates filled with soggy crisps, spilled coffee cups and overturned chairs.

'Mum,' said Freya, catching sight of Clare, dancing and swaying on the kitchen table in the same shorts and red vest top from the night before. The effects of the apple of youth were clearly still going strong.

'Oh Gods, *you* again,' said Clare. 'You're not invited.'

'I just came to see how you are,' said Freya.

'Go away,' said Clare, waving her arms and swigging from a bottle.

Freya went up to her bedroom, her shoes crunching on the rubbish-strewn stairs, and packed a few clothes, books, and the eski in a holdall.

Veronica had told her not to worry about bringing too much as she would be re-styled. *Re-styled!* What a wonderful word to taste on the tongue.

Was this her chance to get famous, too? That would be fun, wouldn't it?

She trudged downstairs, stepping over prone bodies lying in heaps everywhere.

'I need you to sign a consent form,' she said to Clare.

Clare scrawled a signature without reading the letter.

'Turn up the music!' she shrieked. 'Let's PARTY!'

'Bye, Mum,' said Freya. 'I'm off to the Ritz.'

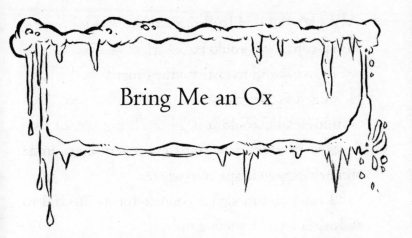

Bring Me an Ox

'Now this,' said the Goddess Freyja, surveying her large suite at the Ritz, the scurrying concierges, the room service and four-poster bed, the stripy mauve and green velvet sofas and tapestried chairs, the floor-to-ceiling windows with views over Green Park, the blue-marbled fireplace, the festooned floral curtains and Turkish carpets, the crystal chandeliers and silver candelabra, 'is more like it. Still *far* too small, but it will do at a pinch.' She reached over and grabbed a handful of chocolates from the overflowing cut-glass bowl on the lacquered black side table, and stuffed them in her mouth.

Thor picked up the chilled champagne bottle and downed it in one gulp.

'What's this stuff called again?' he asked.

'Champagne,' said Freya.

'We wasted our time drinking mead,' said Thor. He picked up the phone.

'Room service?' barked Thor. 'Bring me an ox. Roasted rare. Yes, you heard me, a whole ox. And more champagne.'

'Go easy on the drinking,' said Veronica. 'You have a football try-out coming up.'

'What's football?' asked Thor.

Oh wow. Just in time Veronica remembered her deep-breathing exercises.

'Google it,' she said.

'Freya!' bellowed Thor. 'What's Google? And what's football?'

'I'll show you,' said Freya, sitting down in an ornate gold chair at one of the suite's laptops. She was overwhelmed by the luxury all around her. The thick linen sheets on her enormous bed. A marble bathroom bigger than her bedroom. A wardrobe filled with stylish new clothes. I could get used to all this, she thought, admiring her new Stella McCartney dress. You could forget all about frost giants living in rooms like these.

'Ah, the magic tablet,' said Thor, beaming. He studied the screen. 'So I grab the ball, run, and kill anyone who gets in my way?'

'No,' yelped Freya. 'No killing.'

Thor frowned. 'But that's obviously the best way of keeping the ball.'

Freya looked at Veronica. 'I really don't know—' she faltered.

'Not to worry,' said Veronica, 'we'll get a football coach round for a few lessons this afternoon. My assistant will sort it.'

The Goddess stretched out on the green damask chaise longue and nibbled on more sweets.

'Lay off the chocolates, please,' said Veronica. 'We're taking you round to the top modelling agencies and I'm worried about your hips.'

Freyja looked at Veronica and shoved another handful of chocolates into her mouth.

Her funeral, thought Veronica. She glanced at her list.

'Woden, you'll be auditioning for *FAME: Make Me a Star* so you need to prepare a few songs. The vocal coach will be here in an hour.'

Woden surveyed Freyja's suite.

'Why,' he demanded, 'does she have a fruit bowl in her suite and I don't? Freya. RING THE CONCIERGE.'

Well well, thought Veronica, her new charges had certainly discovered their inner divas way ahead of schedule.

She sighed.

Never mind. At least they can pay for it, she thought.

Where Did You Find This Guy?

Tottenham Hotspur's coach Harry Cray and scout Des Osmond watched the prospective footballer as he raced down the pitch faster than any player they'd ever seen, eluding all attempts to snatch the ball. Harry gasped as the ball sailed into the net, straight past the flailing goalkeeper.

'Where did you find this guy, Des?' he gasped. 'I've never seen anything like it. He makes our boys look like . . . amateurs. My Gods, he's not even out of breath after running like that. He tackles like a tank. He's the whole package – looks, fitness, agility. Except for looks. Must have had a troll for a father. But who cares when he can run like that.' He shook his head.

Des tapped his nose. 'Tip-off. I've got my sources.'

'Has anyone else seen him?'

'Nope. Spurs is the first.'

'And he's *Icelandic*? Do they even *play* footie in Iceland? Ha. Ha. Joke. I've never seen him in their premier league.'

Des shrugged. 'He seems to have sprung out of nowhere. He's never played professionally before. He's a bit sketchy on the rules, it's true, but I've never seen such raw talent and such strength. Maybe it's all the herring they eat there.'

'And his name really is *Thor Bluetooth*?'

The scout nodded.

'Who's his agent? I want him signed TODAY before anyone else sees him.'

Des picked up his mobile and dialled.

Beautiful Beyond the Dreams of Mortals

'Knock 'em dead, honey,' said Veronica, as the black cab pulled up outside a freshly painted building in Floral Street, Covent Garden.

The Goddess looked at Veronica, and her extraordinary cat eyes gleamed.

'She doesn't mean that literally,' said Freya, wincing.

Gods, you could not be too careful with these clients, thought Veronica. Note to self: watch the jokes.

'Just remember what I told you: you are here to *impress* these people,' said Veronica. 'If they don't like you, that's it.'

The Goddess shrugged.

'Everyone loves me,' she said. 'It's the story of my life.'

Veronica watched as Freyja tottered through the snow into Starburst Models, trying not to fall over in her high heels. Freyja had wanted to wear some five-inch studded gold stilettos, but Veronica was firm that until the flaxen-haired Goddess practised walking in high heels, the lower the better. Freya trailed unhappily after her. The Gods had refused to relent: she needed to be with one of them at all times, and Thor was practising on the football pitch and Woden was singing and didn't want to be disturbed.

Veronica and the model booker exchanged big kisses. Freya tried to make herself invisible but the booker didn't appear to even see her.

'This,' said Veronica, 'is my new discovery, Freyja. Don't take too long saying yes, Pierre.'

The skinny booker with floppy brown hair and thick-rimmed black geek glasses eyed Freyja critically. 'Well, you're tall, that's great, and the hair's lovely, and your face is beyond gorgeous, but honey, those hips.'

Freyja stiffened, and drew herself to her full height. She towered over Pierre, who took a step back.

'Don't you "honey" me,' said Freyja. 'I am the Goddess of Beauty, and you're saying I need to . . .

lose weight.' She fixed him with her glittering agate eyes. The man blinked.

'No, no, of course not . . .' he stuttered.

'. . . and that my hips are too *big*?' Freyja's husky voice dropped to a menacing hum. 'My body is strong and powerful. I am beautiful beyond the dreams of mortals.'

'You must have mis-heard me,' said Pierre. 'What was I saying? You're gorgeous. Hips are in this year. Let me just take a few photos. If you could stand by that backdrop.'

Freyja wobbled and tripped.

'Walking can be fixed,' said the booker. 'We'll work on it. You'll be strutting down that catwalk and on the cover of *Vogue* in no time.'

'What's *Vogue*?' said Freyja. 'And why would I walk on cats?'

'You kidding me?'

'Freyja's had a very sheltered upbringing *abroad*,' explained Veronica. 'You know, one of those communities like the Amish,' she added. 'No electricity, no computers, no anything modern.'

'Let's get to work and grab some pics,' said Pierre, taking a few fast snaps.

Freya watched as the Goddess stood still for a moment and gazed at Pierre. Then her presence began to glow and she scorched the room with her glorious beauty.

Pierre put down the camera.

'Wow. Looks great,' he said, awestruck. 'Wow.' He took a few more pictures.

The Goddess scowled.

'What are you pointing at me?'

Pierre looked at Freyja as if she were a lunatic.

'Does she think I'm snatching her soul or something?'

'She's never seen a camera before,' said Freya. 'They're forbidden in her community.'

'What, I am supposed to stand here while he clicks at me?' said the Goddess. '*That's* how I will regain my fame?'

'Yes,' said Veronica.

'Ah, I understand,' said Freyja. 'Instead of carving a statue for one of my temples, he is drawing my picture in the click silver box.'

'Something like that,' said Freya.

'Whatever it takes,' said the Goddess, yawning.

Oh, to Be Famous

Freya stared at the thousands of gaudily dressed, shivering fame-seekers slowly snaking their way round an endless maze of snow-covered crash barriers set up outside the vast O2 arena. There were food trucks, portable loos and patio heaters dotted about, while people with megaphones paraded up and down, organising, prodding, numbering and interviewing.

And that was just the contestants. Thousands more queued to be in the audience, to watch the fame hopefuls strut and fret for their moment in the spotlight.

Woden, in his tunic and hairy cloak and battered blue hat and mad staring eye, fitted right in with all the other flamboyantly dressed wannabes, thought

Freya. Veronica's stylist had decided Woden's 'look' was so original he should keep it for the *Fame* auditions.

Snot, his bodyguard, stood rigidly by his side. Veronica had insisted he could not wear his bear skins, but Snot said he'd kill anyone who tried to remove them, so there he was, scowling and snarling at anyone who approached. Several photographers had already taken his picture but Veronica, shuddering, had refused to let him be interviewed.

Woden surveyed the hordes, all desperately hoping that today fate would be gracious to them and grant them their dreams.

'They look like frozen cattle,' he said. 'Waiting to be slaughtered.'

'Exactly what they are,' said Veronica briskly. 'Luckily not our fate.'

She guided them to a special desk set apart from the others and spoke a few words to the organiser, swaddled in a heavy coat and scarf, who stuck a number on Woden's tunic, a yellow rubber band round his wrist, then pointed them to a door marked Private. The organiser looked enquiringly at Freya. For a mad moment she wanted to holler, 'Me too.

Let me have my chance to be famous. Give me a number and let me on that stage!'

Oh, to be famous. Who cared if it was for singing, dancing – now that would be something, given she had as many left feet as Sleipnir – or just famous for being famous? Wouldn't that serve all the mean kids right when she swanned back to school with her entourage, to present a prize or sing a song, basking in the admiration and the cheers, their faces grotesque with gratitude because she'd brushed past them and somehow *they'd* become more real because they'd breathed the same air as her for a few seconds and touched her coat.

And of course her big fancy houses, and chauffeur-driven cars, and designer clothes and famous friends wouldn't change her a bit. She'd keep it real. She'd still eat fish and chips on the sofa in her multi-million-pound mansion. 'Isn't it amazing how down to Midgard Freya is,' her fans would marvel, 'considering just how very famous and fabulous she is?'

'Well, you know,' Freya would explain modestly in her umpteenth interview, 'I'm just so grateful to all my fans, so proud to be where I am, so humble to be where I am, so proud and yet so humble to be ...' Oh well, she'd have loads of time to work on her soundbites later.

And why the Hel not? Wasn't it true that all you needed was a dream you wanted badly enough for it to come true?

'Freya,' snapped Veronica. 'We're waiting for you.'

Freya's fame reverie went 'pop' and she blushed. How long had she been standing there daydreaming? She followed Woden and Veronica through the magic door. Snot also followed, grimacing.

They entered the vast backstage area of the chilly arena. Everywhere she looked people were singing, dancing, twirling, juggling, texting and chattering. TV monitors let them watch what was happening out front. The place stank of sweat and hairspray and the floor was sticky.

Freya recoiled at the avalanche of weeping and wailing as the spangled rejects hurtled off the stage into the arms of their sobbing friends and family while others high-fived and whooped. It was like being initiated into a grisly secret club of mourners and gladiators.

'*This* is where the bards gather, to compete

for glittering fame and life everlasting?' Woden's lip curled. 'The noise is worse than five hundred drunken warriors clattering their spears and shields.'

'Take a seat over there,' said one of the many clipboard-holding assistants, all wearing radio mikes and burgundy T-shirts with I'LL MAKE YOU A **STAR** embossed on them. He waved to a roped-off area of rows and rows of chairs and tables, packed with nervous contestants and their fluttering families.

'There?' said Woden. 'With the cattle?'

'You haven't made it *yet*, mate,' said the assistant. 'Plenty of time to make diva demands later.'

Wisps of conversation drifted over as they took their seats.

'. . . Always wanted to be a star . . .'

'I'm just following my dream . . .'

'I was born to do this, I can't . . .'

'When I'm famous I'll . . .'

'My nan says . . .'

'Just be glad you've been fast-tracked,' said Veronica. 'You could be waiting in the pens outside for 12 hours. This way you'll go straight in front of the judges.'

'And in front of the world on the magic box?' asked Woden.

'Of course. I'm going out on a limb here for you; I told the producers you were marvellous. They are having you on sight unseen so don't let me down.'

Woden glared at her.

'Now remember, the producers will want to know all about your background, hear your family history, so ladle on the sob stories, okay?' said Veronica. 'I told them a bit about you, not everything of course, and they were *very* interested.'

Probably for the weirdo crazy nutter group, thought Freya. The loonies they put in front of the audience so everyone could laugh at them. She shuddered. Oh Gods what was Woden going to do? Recite his poetry? He'd be laughed out of the arena.

The judges will insult him, and then he'll kill them, thought Freya.

This was not a cheerful scenario.

She looked at him to see if he'd concealed his spear under his cloak. But knowing Woden he could probably still kill people with a look or a charm.

And what would he perform? Would he sing, dance, do magic, raise the dead? Gods, that would be quite a scene, the corpse invasion of the *Fame* set, the audience screaming and struggling to escape while the zombies staggered about . . .

Woden had refused to rehearse or even to discuss what he was planning to perform in front of the judges.

'I sacrificed my eye for wisdom. I have summoned the dead to gain knowledge. I am Lord of Inspiration. I will do what I need to do to regain my fame,' he'd said.

Most likely it would be poetry, thought Freya. But if it were anything like the awful poetry Roskva and Alfi had recited to her on their quest to restore the Gods to youth, then he was in trouble.

'So what's your sob story?' asked Jay the researcher, coming up to Woden.

'My *sob* story?' said Woden. He stood up, towering over the skinny young man, who took a nervous step back.

'Yeah, the story that will make the fans care about ya,' said the researcher, hopping from one red plimsolled foot to the other. 'Dead granny? Divorced parents? Brother with incurable disease?'

'One of my sons killed the other,' said Woden.

'My blind son, Hod, killed my second son, Baldr.'

The researcher stared. 'So, you have a *blind* son, and he *killed* his brother,' said Jay. 'That's heavy. What, like on purpose?' he gasped.

'An accident,' said Woden.

'Gods,' said the researcher, writing furiously. 'So, were they like, little kids when this happened?'

'No,' said Woden.

'Wow,' said the researcher. 'I like it. Really Eddic.' He went off to the next table to interview a scary-looking woman with teased blue hair, wearing a bathrobe and high-heeled shoes.

'Great story about the kids,' said Veronica. 'The producers will love that. Make sure you dedicate your performance to the dead one.'

*

Oh Gods, thought Freya. How much longer would they have to wait? It felt like she'd spent her whole life in this place.

Woden stared off into the distance. He looked like a warrior who had found himself trapped in a sewing circle.

'I'm going to be a star. End of,' announced a balding man sitting nearby squeezed into a leotard.

'That's not my dream, it's my reality.' Then he repeated, 'I'm going to be a star. I'm going to be a star. My album will be a massive number-one bestseller. This is my fate. This is my fate.'

'It will be your fate to be drowned head first in a barrel of fish guts if you don't shut up,' snarled Woden.

Veronica looked pained.

'Snapping at people is not going to win you any fans,' said Freya.

'I'll talk to people any way I like,' said Woden.

'Save that for when you're famous again, then you can be as horrible as you want,' said Veronica. 'But right now you need to woo people. You can't just smite them into submission.'

Woden looked sullen.

'But he's got to be himself . . .' said Freya.

She trailed off. If Woden were himself he'd never get a single vote.

'And you're going to have to smile occasionally,' said Veronica.

'Smile?' said Woden fiercely. '*Smile?* I'm the All-Father. The Wand-Wielder. The God of Victory. I don't *smile*.'

'I'm sorry,' said Veronica, 'but you have to be appealing. Just like us, but better than us, born to rule but, you know, caring.'

'No I don't,' said Woden. 'I'm a God. It's enough that people are scared of me and do what they're told.'

Veronica pretended she hadn't heard.

'We have to practise that smile,' she said.

'No.'

'If you don't smile no one will vote for you, and this is all about getting fans,' said Veronica. 'Isn't it?'

Woden's mouth twitched.

'That wasn't a smile. That was someone with rigor mortis,' said Veronica.

Woden bared his teeth.

'The judges will think you intend to eat them,' said Veronica. 'Smile.'

Woden curled his lips. He looked like a wolf about to chow down on a slaughtered deer.

'It is fortunate to be favoured with praise and popularity,' said Woden. 'It is dire luck to be dependent on the feelings of men.'

'You haven't mentioned his talent,' said Freya timidly. 'His talent will make him stand out. And he's . . . unique.'

'Originality is good, and reciting poetry is certainly that,' said Veronica. 'And you've got plenty of confidence, but . . . not sure about your attitude.'

Well. She'd worked with less promising material before, and had managed to mould the sullen clay into something approaching shiny gold – at least for a few moments. She wasn't the best fame-maker in the business for nothing. She glanced at her notes.

'Oh yes, what stage name are you going to use? We're holding back Woden for the big reveal.'

Woden considered.

'I am blessed with many names. I am Draugadrottin, Lord of the Dead. Valfodr, Father of the Slain. Hangi, the Hanged One. Vidurr, the Killer.'

'I'm getting a theme here, but not a very alluring one,' said Veronica. 'Anything a bit more cheerful?'

'Itreker, Splendid Ruler?'

'Too vain.'

'Audun, Wealth-friend?'

'Perfect for when you launch your get-rich-quick schemes, but not now.'

'Sidskeggr, Drooping Beard? Hrossharsgrani, Horse-Hair Moustache?'

'Too silly,' said Veronica. 'We're talking worldwide fans here.'

Freya thought. She'd had to memorise all of Woden's names once for a school competition, but unfortunately had come 53rd . . .

'Oski?' she said. The name he'd told Clare.

'Wished-for,' said Veronica. 'I like it.'

'Oski,' said Woden.

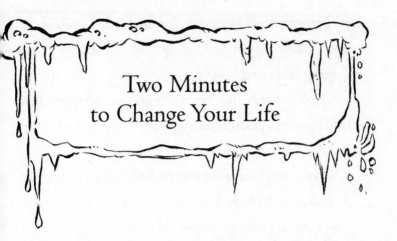

Two Minutes
to Change Your Life

The audience waited expectantly, then the four judges, in a hail of lasers and lights, took their seats.

'Welcome to *FAME: Make Me a Star*, the show where talent makes dreams come true,' gushed the host, Fliss Griffiths, a former reality TV star turned presenter.

Freya couldn't sit still she was so nervous. She'd bitten all her nails. She paced the backstage holding area, heading back to her seat and then wheeling out and going to the loo one absolutely last final time. So much depended on this. Her life, and the lives of everyone around them, if they only knew.

'You're on!' hissed the stage manager, pushing contestant 2,724 onto the stage.

'I want to follow my dreams and be a singer,'

announced the sweaty man in his 40s. 'I used to be a postman, but the job was getting in the way of my singing and song writing.'

'Not getting in the way enough,' snapped the cruel judge, Darren, a soap star who'd had a hit record in 5008.

'My gran got a message from the Gods telling me to audition so here I am,' said a baton-twirling girl. 'I've been waiting my whole life for this.'

Four nos from the judges.

'I'm singing for my mum, who passed away last year,' said a wood-chopping puppeteer.

'That really pulled at my heartstrings,' said Bitty Kitty, the soppy girl-band singer.

The a cappella choir sang their version of a recent number one.

'Out of this world,' said Barry, the useless judge. 'You're through to the next round.'

Then there were the opera rappers. The mini-rockettes. The Singing Chef. So many competitors that after a time they all blended into one. Freya's head ached.

'You smashed that,' said Bitty Kitty to the twins with their dancing dogs. More tears and screams than Freya had heard in her life.

The numbers ticked down, getting closer and closer to Woden.

Next up were a hip-hop marching band.

'We're called Sure Thing because that's what we are. A sure thing. Our destiny is to be stars.'

'I think you need a new fortune teller,' said Darren.

Next up was a dancing juggler.

'I'm dedicating this performance to my dead horse, Rooster,' said the juggler. 'And to my granddad who is having a hernia operation.'

'I just love you all so much,' gushed the next contestant, a yodelling ballerina. 'Thanks to everyone who votes for me, because without you I am nothing.'

Right up before Woden were two duelling trombonists.

'You and the trombones owned that stage,' gushed Bitty Kitty. 'Wow.'

'Can the stage be bought?' said Woden, bristling. 'Why didn't you tell me?'

'It's just an expression,' said Veronica.

'You're up next,' hissed the Assistant. '3-2-1 — you're on.'

And he pushed Woden through the curtains.

The God stood blinking and scowling in the flashing lights. Unlike every other contestant, who had tried to engage with the judges and audience, he did and said nothing. He just stood there, frozen. He looked like a bewildered sailor, shipwrecked in some far-off land, scanning the horizon for monsters heading his way. The audience tittered.

Freya gripped her chair and moaned softly. Veronica grabbed her arm.

'Whatever happens, let me handle it,' she hissed. 'He's on his own now.'

I don't think I can watch this, thought Freya.

'What's your name?' asked Barry.

'Call me Oski,' said Woden.

A ripple went through the audience.

'We know that Oski is one of the All-Father's many names — your parents must have thought you were pretty special when they named you,' said Darren.

'Only a fool chatters,' said Woden. He looked belligerently at the judge.

Veronica sucked in her breath.

'And why did you audition, Oski?' asked the useless judge.

'To remind the ungrateful world about the immortal Gods who gave them life, the Gods they have forgotten.'

'O-kay,' said Barry.

'What's your dream?' asked Darren.

'World domination,' said Woden.

'You want to make it worldwide? What a goal, ladies and gentlemen,' burbled Fliss.

'What inspired you to audition today?' asked Lila, a kittenish woman with big red hair tied in a swinging ponytail and heavily made-up eyes, who'd won the show two years before.

Woden looked at her as if she were a snail he was about to squish.

'To regain my bright fame.'

Lila looked surprised.

'. . . and change your destiny?' she prompted.

'No one, not even I, can change my destiny,' said Woden. 'What is fated will come to pass.'

Oh Gods, Woden, lighten up, thought Freya. You're trying to make people worship and admire you, not put them off.

'Oh,' said Lila.

'So, Oski, how are you feeling right now?' said the host, Fliss.

Freya held her breath.

She knew he'd be feeling like hurling his spear at Fliss and setting fire to the rafters.

Woden glared. 'None of your business,' he snarled.

The audience gasped. Then they started to boo.

Woden fixed them with his one eye. They immediately fell silent.

'So, can I ask how you lost your eye? Was it an accident?' asked Fliss.

'I traded it for wisdom,' said Woden.

Fliss stepped back. 'Whew, that's intense,' she said. 'Was it worth the sacrifice?'

'What do you think?' said Woden.

'Like all the contestants, you must have been on an amazing personal journey,' said Lila. 'What can you tell us about your journey here?'

'I came over Bifrost of course,' said Woden.

Fliss laughed and flicked her tousled blonde hair. 'Isn't he a character, ladies and gentlemen. Of course, being on stage here tonight in front of millions of people feels like going from Midgard to Asgard.'

Woden fixed her with his baleful eye.

'Before you show us your talent, is there anyone you want to thank?' she asked.

'No,' said Woden.

'Not even your mum?'

Woden's eye flashed.

'My . . . mother? Bestla?'

'Lovely name,' beamed Fliss. 'You know, your wonderful mum who helped and encouraged you and made all this possible?'

'Why should I want to thank her?' said Woden. 'What did she ever do for me? Haven't seen her for millennia.'

'Of course, she must be so proud of you,' said Fliss, ignoring what Woden had just said.

Woden frowned.

'I doubt it.'

Freya groaned. Thank someone, she thought. Anyone . . .

'I thank the immortal, Almighty Gods,' said Woden suddenly. 'For whom no praise is enough. To the Gods, givers of victory, to Woden, source of poetry and power, magician and mage.'

The arena was silent.

A look of alarm flickered across Fliss's face, then she recovered herself.

'Well, that makes a change from thanking your old granny,' she said. 'Well done, Oski. Always good to be reminded of religion in this material age.'

Woden looked as if he would like to smite her.

No smiting! thought Freya. Remember. You promised.

'You've got two minutes to change your life,' said Barry. 'Go for it.'

Woden stood for a moment, looking over the hushed audience.

Freya could scarcely breathe. Please don't let his poetry be booed off the stage, she thought.

Then Woden hurled his microphone into the wings.

Freya jumped. No one would hear him. Out of the corner of her eye she saw a stage hand racing backstage holding a spare mike.

'I dedicate my performance to Woden, source of all inspiration, All-Father, Mighty One, Bringer of Victory!' he boomed. His unamplified voice ricocheted around the vast building.

And then, without stopping, he started to sing,

softly and quietly, and it was as if a spell had been cast over everyone. His beautiful voice poured out like salted caramel.

Then he began to whirl and leap around the stage, in a heart-stopping, haunting, frenzy of music and song, unlike anything she had ever heard before: melodic, magical, rhythmic, hypnotic. His voice harsh and pebbly one moment, velvety the next.

A murmur cascaded round the auditorium, then the roaring audience leapt to its feet, shouting and cheering. Freya was swept up in the hysteria. To her surprise she found herself joining the others, screaming, 'Oski! Oski! Oski!' as the stadium erupted in flashing lights from thousands of camera phones.

The judges rose to their feet.

'That is the most incredible performance I have ever seen in my life,' stuttered Lila.

'You're individual, you're unpredictable, you've got charisma; I predict a huge future for you,' gasped Darren.

'We love the image – the cloak, the hat, the hair,' enthused Barry. 'You're new, you're different, you're a one-off original – Let's hear it for Oski!'

And as the stomping, screaming audience chanted

his name and held out their hands yearning to touch him, as they looked up at him with ecstatic faces twisted in awe, Freya saw Woden shine and shimmer and his presence and power fill the auditorium, and she thought, thank the Gods, we're saved.

Meanwhile

A howling hiss, a creaking crunch shattered the silent silver world. Then a gigantic frozen fist punched through the rippling surface and the sheer ice cliffs collapsed into the sea.

PART 3
CELEBRITY GODS

The multi-media collage of modern life
makes it hard for an upcoming god to
establish himself without a web presence.

Grayson Perry

Die for Me

Wow, thought Veronica. Wow.

A few months into her publicity campaign for the Gods, and things, if she said so herself (if you didn't blow your own trumpet who would?) couldn't be going better. Not that she wanted to tempt fate, but then, she wasn't superstitious. If it was fated, it happened. If it wasn't, it didn't. End of.

Woden had won *FAME: Make Me a Star* by acclamation – the betting shops had stopped taking money on him winning after that storming first audition. Votes had poured in. And every vote seemed to make him stronger. Each time Woden was mobbed in the streets, or greeted by screaming, fainting fans, he seemed to grow a little taller. More powerful. Less human.

More, dare she say it, divine.

Woden's record 'Die for Me' had gone straight in at number one and was the fastest selling single ever to go platinum. The press adored him. Photographers followed him everywhere. He had 30 million Twitter followers . . . and counting. (Too bad, Lady Gaga!) Twitter, the Geiger counter of fame, was going nuclear. She'd already had to hire a full-time tweeter for him. He had 50 million Facebook friends. His fan site, *Gods-Children.com* got millions of hits every day.

Woden had taken to dropping by his Fanes on Sundays. Amazing, thought Veronica, one mention in *ICE* magazine that he was religious and the fans – she meant worshippers – crammed the empty Fanes just in case Woden showed up.

Last week there'd been a riot when he'd arrived at one in Kensington, so now he was appearing with snarling bodyguards wearing bear skins. She'd read in the *Daily Mail* that one of them had threatened to kill someone who got too close. Snot, presumably. Well, it all added to the mystique and the hype surrounding him.

Thor had already been proclaimed the greatest

footballer ever to play in the premier league. What a moment that was, after his triumphant first game, when the fans all chanted 'Thor! Thor! Thor!' and Thor had picked up his hammer with one hand and whirled it above his head as if it were a willow twig, to the opening chorus of Woden's number one hit.

'I love this game!' he'd shouted, dancing around the pitch as the fans roared. 'Even more fun than bashing giants!'

And as for the Goddess Freyja, she'd been on the cover of *Elle* and *Marie Claire*, done all the big catwalk shows and was a regular fixture in *ICE* and the gossip columns. The picture of her yawning that Pierre had taken had been on every billboard in Britain. It went viral on YouTube, featured in spoof montages (Freyja yawning in front of the Taj Mahal; yawning while dinosaurs stalked her; yawning beside the Queen; yawning while Mo Farah won gold at the 5012 Olympics; yawning at the Royal Wedding).

Of course, it wasn't all plain sailing. It never was with fame-seekers. There was the terrible incident when Thor got tripped up, picked up his opponent and hurled him across the pitch, screaming that no one would ever set eyes on the scumbag again. The player was still in hospital. It had taken all her skill to spin that as an unlucky accident.

There'd been a hint of a fight in a London nightclub, but she'd quickly hushed that up in exchange for exclusive pictures of Thor's glorious new mansion, complete with indoor and outdoor pools, glass lift to the master-bedroom suite, waterproof TVs in every bathroom, a gym, cinema room, spa, sauna, steam room and armoury. (That was a bit unusual, but no weirder than many of her clients, with their gift-wrapping rooms and basement bars.) Well, they couldn't stay in the Ritz forever, could they, not after Woden's unfortunate room-trashing incident (hushed up) and the brawl in the lobby. The tens of thousands of screaming fans camped out in front of the hotel every night, blocking Piccadilly and spilling over the permanent crash barriers into the hotel lobby, hadn't helped either.

Getting them famous friends and being seen in the right A-list company was proceeding nicely: what amazing coverage Thor's birthday party at the Ivy Club had had. An invitation to dinner at

Buckingham Palace, or a weekend at Windsor, was just a matter of time.

Long may it last.

If only it wasn't so fiendishly cold.

Meanwhile

All over the icy landscape, frost-covered giants erupted through the cracking glaciers. The sea reared up, twisting and writhing, splashing them with sleet.

The largest frost giant stood on creaking, tree-trunk legs and roared, spitting shards of icicles, sharp as daggers, from its mouth.

The shifting ice groaned beneath their stomping feet, as the massed army of giants lumbered towards Bifrost through billowing sheets of snow, exhaling their blizzard breath.

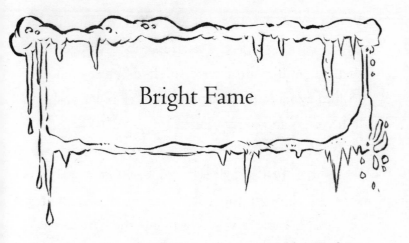

Bright Fame

Somehow, thought Freya, as she trudged home from the corner shop through the mounds of drifting snow, trying not to slip on the icy pavement, it wasn't going to plan. Thanks to her, the Gods had regained their bright fame, idolised and worshipped as never before. And yet they seemed in no rush to reveal their true selves. Or to return to Asgard. Or to stop the frost giants. Last time Freya had even seen the Gods – and that was a while ago – she'd noticed the glossy estate agent brochures strewn everywhere. What was *that* about, she'd wondered.

Since then, Thor had actually bought a mansion with his massive football earnings, and she'd heard that all three Gods were living there, protected by 24-hour security guards, crash barriers, and Snot.

When they'd left – okay, been kicked out of the Ritz – no one had said anything about her joining them in millionaires' row, so she'd returned home to find Clare still out clubbing every night and the house a tip and party central.

Why weren't the Gods doing anything, she thought, as hail and sleet pelted her. The world had shivered through the coldest autumn and winter on record. Now it was April, and the Thames was freezing over. Freya had tried phoning them on their bling-bling, diamond-encrusted smart phones, yet she always went straight to answerphone. Were they avoiding her, she wondered? Or just too busy with parties and famous friends and personal appearances?

They're our Gods, they must know what they're doing, thought Freya, her teeth chattering. I'm a kid. Shy. Funny-looking. Not even near the top of my class. Picked last for team sports. What can I do?

She passed the bus stop, covered in images of Thor advertising running shoes, and the newsagent. A headline caught her eye. In fact, several headlines. She stopped, transfixed.

Oh no, she thought. Please no.

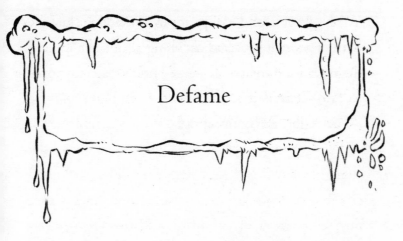

Defame

Veronica opened the papers. They did not make pleasant reading. Freyja, her new supermodel, was accused of cheating on several boyfriends. That's when she wasn't busy shoplifting. Thor, Veronica's new footballing superstar, was accused of having kidnapped two children and keeping them as virtual slaves. There was a lurid kiss-and-tell, in fact several kiss-and-tells, about her rock superstar Woden. The internet was buzzing with horrible gossip.

Where did all of these scandalous stories come from, she wondered? Where did these lie-smiths get their facts? Who was spreading these shocking rumours about the Gods? Who wanted to destroy their reputation? And why?

Who was de-faming them?

Her phone rang, the piercing alarm tone she used for her most important clients.

Veronica grabbed it.

A voice screeched in her ear.

'Sit tight, I'm coming right away,' she said.

Meanwhile

Up in Asgard, beneath the vast, arching branches of the giant ash tree, Yggdrasil, was a circle of ivory-white stone thrones, their seats worn smooth. The Gods and Goddesses were gathered there in Council, around a glimmering pool of blue-black water.

'*What* are they doing?' said Njord. 'Every time I sit in Woden's High Seat to peer into Midgard I see them. The Terrible One, the Father of Battle, is singing and leaping about, or signing pieces of parchment for clamouring mortals. Thor is running up and down a field chasing an inflated pig's bladder, and my daughter Freyja is – I'm not sure what she's doing, strutting up and down a walkway each time in different clothes, while people point flashing objects at her.'

'Have they fallen under a troll's spell?' asked Woden's wife, Frigg.

'And now the frost giants are on the march,' said Heimdall. 'The Wolf Age and the Ice Age will be upon us.'

'What are we going to do?' said Sif.

The Immortals sat in silence, heads bowed.

Above them the leaves of the World Tree shimmered in a sudden gust of wind. The great branches swayed and creaked.

The Gods shivered.

Gods Can Do
What They Like

There were some advantages, thought Freya, as she let herself into the cold, dirty house, stomping the snow off her scuffed shoes, to having a mother who was rarely home. No one to make her go to school, clean her room, or stop her from going out. On the other hand, she was getting a little tired of eating cereal all the time and the milk being off and having to go through Clare's pockets for cash when she was snoring off the excesses of a hard night's partying.

The TV was blaring loudly in the sitting room. Freya walked in to find Clare with dyed pink and orange hair sprawled on the sofa in her filthy hobnail boots watching the Shopping Channel, eating crisps, fiddling with her nose ring and listening to music on her headphones.

'You still here?' said Clare, rolling her eyes. She looked absolutely ridiculous in laddered black tights, a silver sequin micro mini skirt and tight red T-shirt with a picture of a man sticking out his studded tongue.

'I live here,' said Freya. She looked at Clare's arm.

'Mum!' wailed Freya. 'You haven't gone and got a . . . tattoo. Ick.'

'So what if I have?' said Clare. 'And stop calling me Mum.'

'It's horrible,' said Freya, looking with distaste at the hissing snake wrapped round a wolf's skull writhing all over her mother's freckly wrist.

'Then don't look at it,' said Clare. 'Gods, I'm bored. Why is there never anything to eat in this stupid house?'

'Because you haven't gone shopping and I'm busy trying to save the world,' snapped Freya.

Clare rolled her eyes. 'Oh yeah, Supergirl. Whatever. Wake me when it's over.'

When oh when would that apple wear off, thought Freya.

'By the way something weird happened today,' said Clare, biting her nails. 'This priest guy, Karl, came round, said I hadn't been to Fane in ages and he and the Throng were worried about me. I say, *me*, but I didn't have a clue what he was talking about. Why would I be hanging around a Fane? I mean, obvs, if Oski is making a personal appearance, then yeah, but otherwise . . .' she yawned elaborately.

'Did he recognise you?' asked Freya.

'What do you mean, *recognise* me? Like from *Crimewatch*? No. He asked me to tell Clare he'd stopped by. Like I said, weird.'

Freya looked at her mum, who for a moment seemed uncertain and disoriented.

'The world is full of weirdos, including you, loser,' said Clare.

There was a frantic pounding on Freya's front door.

'Oh Gods, *him* again,' said Clare. 'Tell him I'm out.' She plugged in her earphones and closed her eyes.

Freya opened the door, scrambling to think of a convincing lie.

It wasn't Karl. It was Alfi and Roskva. They looked pale and windswept, as if they had run all the way from Asgard to Midgard.

'Thank Gods you're here,' said Freya, hugging

them both. At last. She wasn't alone any more, trying to be the grown-up to a teenage mum.

Only Alfi hugged her in return. His face felt frozen. Roskva held back, stiff as always.

'Where's Woden? Where's Thor? Where's Freyja?' they clamoured.

'Probably being interviewed by *ICE* magazine or at a nightclub,' said Freya grimly.

'What?' said Alfi.

'The Gods have sent us to fetch them back to Asgard immediately,' said Roskva.

'The frost giants are coming,' they said in unison. 'They've broken free.'

Freya breathed deeply. She hustled them into the kitchen past her mother and shut the door.

'What's going on?' said Roskva. 'The Gods are frightened. There's been no word from the All-Father for months.'

'What's happened to them?' asked Alfi.

'I don't know,' said Freya. 'I thought fame would make them powerful again, and it has, but they are – changed. Drugged. I think I may have done something terrible.' She stopped speaking, horrified at the words escaping her mouth.

'It's not your fault,' said Alfi.

'Then whose is it?' said Roskva. 'The frost giants—'

'They wanted fame,' said Freya. 'And I got them fame.'

'And it's obviously gone completely to their heads,' said Roskva.

'They're worshipped everywhere,' said Freya. 'They're strong and powerful and admired again. But I think all they care about now is whose fame shines brightest.'

'They never much cared about people before, you know,' said Roskva. 'We worshipped them because they terrified us. Thor could have wiped out my family with a snap of his fingers.'

'They created us, and then forgot about us,' said Freya.

'We've always been the playthings of the Gods,' said Roskva.

'But they need us as much as we need them,' said Freya. 'I see that now. In fact, they need us *more* than we need them.'

Freya shivered at the thought. Alfi blanched.

'Don't *say* that,' he hissed. 'You're wrong. Just wait

till the giants come, and see whether we need the Gods or not.'

'Gods don't exist unless people worship them,' said Freya. 'Well, they worship them now. But for how long? The Gods will soon be yesterday's news unless they do more to merit their fame. Already the newspapers have started to tear them down. Don't they owe us *something* for our worship?'

'The Gods can do what they like,' said Roskva. 'They can help us or not. They can build. They can destroy.'

They looked at one another. Freya saw the terror in their eyes.

'We've got to warn them the frost giants are coming,' said Freya. 'They'll listen to you.'

Meanwhile

The giants lumbered across Asgard's wide plains, roaring and howling, blasting the green lands with their billowing frost, their hissing breath.

The Gods' Delusion

Thousands of fans wearing woolly hats and winter coats huddled outside the high stone walls of Thor's gated mansion on Archpriests Avenue. The noisy crowd, though numerous, was smaller than the screaming hordes which had once gathered outside the Ritz.

Freya saw a familiar glaring face lurking at the back.

'Snot,' she said. 'What are you doing out here?'

'Woden has made me redundant,' said Snot. 'Whatever that means. My services are no longer required, he said. Modernising, he said. I am one of Woden's berserkers. I am one of the chosen warriors of Valhalla. How can I no longer be needed?'

Roskva patted his arm awkwardly. 'Stay close,' she said. 'The giants are coming.'

Snot's black wolf-eyes gleamed.

Freya, Roskva and Alfi pushed their way through the tightly packed fans to the entrance, guarded by two security men dressed as berserkers.

Freya's name was still on the approved list of visitors, and the electronic, wrought-iron security gates opened to admit them. More guards lurked inside, patrolling the frosty manicured lawns leading to the mansion's colonnaded threshold. Swivelling cameras tracked them as they walked through the massive front door.

'We have to see Oski,' said Freya to the smartly dressed assistant standing in the mirrored entrance hall. 'It's urgent.'

Roskva and Alfi gaped at the opulence, the pink crystal chandelier dripping from the second floor, the plush carpets, the bronze statues of boars pawing the ground. The hallway was bigger than her entire house, thought Freya. Several other people milled about, one man with bulging biceps wearing jogging trousers, the others in business suits. One woman pushed a large rack of designer clothes. Another lugged a suitcase full of make-up.

'Join the queue,' said the assistant.

Thor's bellowing could be heard echoing through the building.

'Who is trying to besmirch our bright fame?' he roared from somewhere in the house.

'They're in a meeting,' said another assistant. 'Take a seat,' he added, pointing to one of the sumptuous cream sofas.

'No,' said Roskva. 'I told you it's urgent. Tell them that Roskva and Alfi are here.'

'He's expecting us,' said Alfi.

The assistant hesitated, then went upstairs and opened one of the massive closed doors.

'He said to wait,' said the assistant, descending. 'Can I get you a glass of water?'

'*Wait?*' said Roskva. '*Wait?!* May the trolls take you! May your end be horrible. May you never enter Valhalla.'

'There's no need to swear,' said the young man, frowning.

'We don't have time to wait,' said Freya.

Roskva, Alfi and Freya leapt up, dashed upstairs and ran through the closed double doors before the startled assistant could stop them.

'All-Father. We're back. The giants are coming,' they shouted as they burst in.

The startled Gods stopped pacing the marble floor of the sumptuous black, white and gold room. Freya caught a glimpse of extensive snow-covered gardens and iced pools through the floor-to-ceiling French doors.

'Sit down and shut up,' said Veronica. Honestly. How was she supposed to crisis manage with all these interruptions?

'But . . . but, we have—' said Freya.

'Be quiet,' ordered Thor.

Roskva and Alfi cowered.

'Everyone, stay calm,' said Veronica. 'First of all, we'll deny everything. I mean really, enslaving two children?'

Thor didn't look at her.

'*What*? You did?' said Veronica. 'No, stop, I don't want to know,' she continued, glancing at Roskva and Alfi. 'We'll deny it anyway. Then we'll threaten libel and demand a retraction. Plus, I can make a deal with the papers. Offer them access to you, in exchange for sitting on any other stories.'

'*More* stories?' shouted Woden. The ravens perched

on his shoulders jumped in fright. His eye was impenetrable behind his aviator sunglasses. 'Who defames us? Who is trying to kill us by destroying our reputation and soiling our names? Who? Why?'

A name floated unspoken in the room.

Roskva broke the silence.

'Could it be the Wolf's father?'

'The Wolf's father?' hissed Freya.

'Loki,' said Alfi.

Loki.

Freya felt a stab of fear. Loki, the trickster, who had tried to thwart her in Hel, who had stolen Idunn and her apples of youth and almost caused the Gods to die along with her. No one had seen him since Freya had transformed herself into a falcon and left him behind in Hel, cursing her as she flew off. Had he followed her to Midgard?

'We'll find him and shut his mouth,' said the Goddess Freyja.

'We lost fame once. Now fate has given us a second chance, we will not lose it again,' said Thor. He was decked in his new lightning bolt tracksuit range with his name emblazoned back and front in huge block letters.

'We now know the emptiness of life without fame and worship,' said Woden. 'We can never go back to how we were before.'

'I feel young. I feel rejuvenated,' said the Goddess Freyja. 'We can't lose our fame again. I couldn't bear it.'

'I said I could *make* you famous,' said Veronica. 'I never promised I could *keep* you famous. People are fickle, and there are new celebrities coming all the time. That's the way of the world.'

'I'll kill you if I don't get the cover of *GQ* next week,' snarled Thor.

'No, because I'll kill her first if *I* don't get the cover,' snapped Woden.

Veronica backed away.

'I'm much more useful to you alive than dead,' she said.

'Lords, the frost giants are coming,' interrupted Roskva.

'The other Gods need you back in Asgard right now,' said Alfi.

'Loki is on the loose,' said Roskva.

'Listen to them,' said Freya. 'Please.'

Woden waved his hand.

'In a minute,' said Woden, leafing through the latest issue of *ICE*. His face flickered in annoyance.

'Veronica,' he said. 'Why is there a three-page spread about Thor, and only a small picture of me leaving that launch party?'

The Goddess snatched the magazine. A satisfied smile spread across her face. 'My holiday snaps look good,' she said. 'But maybe I should have worn a different bikini. What do you think?' she asked Woden. 'The green stripes or the gold halter-top?'

'Who cares about your bikinis,' thundered Woden. 'I had two pages last month, a photo spread, and a featured interview, and now I have a paragraph about looking tired and jowly. Well, whoever made that decision will regret it. I will not be defamed. I'm taking my spear straight round—'

'All-Father, please, the frost giants are coming,' interrupted Freya. 'You must—'

Roskva poked her hard in the ribs.

Freya gulped.

'Did you speak, thrall?' hissed the Goddess.

'Did you say we *must*?' thundered Thor.

Woden waved his hand at her. 'We'll deal with them,' he said. 'And with Loki. But first things first.

Veronica!' he barked. 'I need a facial before the red carpet tonight.'

'I'm not happy with the clothes they sent over for me,' said Thor. 'I'm Thor, not some semi-demi D-list celebrity.'

Freya stared at the Gods gazing at their reflections and gabbling into their phones. Facials? Photo shoots? Their new fame had intoxicated them.

The Goddess glanced at her wrist. She was wearing, Freya noticed, a new, diamond-encrusted watch.

'Must dash, my personal shopper is picking me up at 2,' she trilled. 'I'm having a complete wardrobe makeover.'

'Did you pay for that watch?' asked Veronica.

Freyja stuck out her newly plumped-up lips.

'I don't have to pay, I'm the Goddess Freyja,' she said. 'Mortals pay me tribute.'

'You can't just steal things,' said Veronica. 'If that gets in the papers, your reputation.'

'That's your problem, not mine,' said Freyja. 'Are the photographers still outside?'

Veronica went to the window and peered out.

'There's a huge crowd of them waiting,' she said. 'And loads of fans, too.'

Freyja beamed.

'Waiting for *me*, I expect.'

'I think you'll find that *I* am the one they're waiting for,' said Woden.

'Well let's just see,' said Freyja, sashaying to the window to an explosion of clicks and ear-shattering screams.

'We love you, Freyja!' squealed a gaggle of giggling schoolgirls.

'Over here, Freyja,' one photographer yelled.

'To me, to me,' called another.

'Look this way,' shouted a third.

'How are you, Freyja?' hollered a man in the crowd.

'Fabulous,' she giggled, leaning out of the window and pouting at the cameras, oblivious to the bitter cold.

'What about those stories in the paper today – any comment?' shrieked a reporter.

'Is it true about the shoplifting?' they chorused.

Freyja slammed the window shut.

She came back to the chaise longue, looking grim.

'Now, I've been in discussions with a cable channel about doing a reality TV show about you all to tie in with the big reveal,' said Veronica. 'Potentially *very* exciting.' (Though whether they will still be interested after all those horrible stories remains to be seen, she didn't add.) '*At Home with the Gods* or *Asgard behind the Golden Door*. It will be an incredible marketing tool for all your merchandise: we're thinking hammer amulets endorsed by Thor, so extra powerful, those will be luxury items, flax linen sheets – *Sleep like the Gods* – and we might think about a diffusion range, and Woden raven soft toys, and some children's books – every publisher is interested, naturally, and charms—'

'No charms,' said Woden. 'I have to keep some exclusive powers for myself.'

'You're right,' said Veronica smoothly, making a note, 'and Freyja, we will need to have a separate discussion about a hair and make-up line – I think *Goddess* would be a great brand, and it gives us loads of taglines: 'Look Like a Goddess!' 'Smell Like a Goddess!' 'Dress Like a Goddess,' etc., you get the idea. If you'll just take a peek at some preliminary sketches for your first perfume bottle, which we'd like to call, obviously, *Freyja*.' Something seductive, like 'Je t'aime. Freyja.'

Woden snorted.

'You know we hardly need the money.'

Freyja yawned.

'Speak for yourself. I can't have enough gold.'

'Yes, of course,' said Veronica, 'but you *do* want fans, and your millions of fans all want a part of you. It just spreads your fame.'

'I'm feeling stronger and stronger,' said Woden.

'Good, because I have to warn you . . . it won't last forever. There are always new gods, new idols, waiting in the wings. This month it's you, next — who knows?'

She let the phrase hover in the air. It was always good to keep clients on their toes, let them know they had to work hard to stay on top of the churning pile and kick away the fame-seekers scrabbling desperately beneath them.

'And of course, we should release a calendar for the Yule Festival. Pictures of you with assorted baked goods. We can call it *Bringing the World Back to Woden One Biscuit at a Time.*

Woden made a face. 'Isn't that beneath my dignity?'

'You need to at least *fake* being humble and in touch,' said Veronica. 'Keep it real.'

'I have *never* been humble,' said Woden. 'I am the All-Father. Don't ever forget that.'

'What about the frost giants?' pleaded Freya.

'I said later,' said Woden.

Dooda-loo Dooda-loo honked one of Veronica's phones. She answered, walking into the corner to speak quietly.

'*Glory* want a story about who you're dating, Freyja,' said Veronica.

'None of their business.'

'I think we should find you a nice footballer,' said Veronica.

Freyja frowned.

'Look, if you want to keep people worshipping you, we have to keep feeding them stories,' said Veronica.

'Make something up then,' said Freyja. 'I don't want to get a bad reputation.'

Thor snorted.

'What?' said Freyja.

'Bit late for that, don't you think?' said Thor, smirking.

'You're just jealous because I'm more famous than you now,' said Freyja, tossing her luxurious curls. 'Did you know I'm going to be the new face of *Lustre* shampoo?'

'Come on, focus, people,' said Veronica. 'Thor, let's discuss the sponsorships and a possible appearance on *Desert Island Celebrity*.'

'No way,' said Thor. 'That show's for has-beens.'

Veronica paused.

'I know, it's not *exactly* A-list stuff, but we have to do everything we can to keep you in the public eye for as long as we can. Look what it did for Peter Andre: once he couldn't open a supermarket; now he owns them. Woden, there's the interview tomorrow for the *The Times*, so I've prepared a list of possible questions and of course the movie premiere tonight—'

'Can I just say—' began Freya.

'What's the film?' asked Woden.

'Uhhhm, it's called *Gross-Out Weekend: The Whole Salami,'* said Veronica.

'*Gross-Out Weekend: The Whole Salami?*' repeated Thor. 'That doesn't sound like a major release.'

'Okay, it's probably not gonna win film of the year, but there will be photographers there, and we need to keep your faces in the papers,' said Veronica smoothly. She decided not to tell them that she'd had to argue hard for the invitations after the morning's disastrous headlines. 'Anyhow, I've arranged for the limousines . . .'

'How big is my limousine?' said Woden. 'By rights, mine must be the biggest.'

'I'm the most famous now,' said Freyja, 'so I need the biggest limo. Is that clear?'

'I'm more famous than you,' said Thor. 'Always was, and always will be, so I insist—'

'Veronica, I order you to *measure* the cars when they arrive,' said Woden. 'If mine isn't the biggest I'm not going.'

Freya thought her head would explode if she listened to this a moment longer. Was this what fame meant to them now? Whatever happened to regaining their powers to fight the frost giants?

'Stop! Stop!' screamed Freya. 'What are you doing? Going to parties? Stuffing your faces, buying junk, showing off? What's happened to you? What happened to being famous for great and glorious deeds? The frost giants are coming to destroy the world and you're arguing about who's got the biggest car.

The trolls take your bragging and boasting.'

Freya paused for a moment, breathing hard. The Gods stared open-mouthed at her.

'Freya, stop,' said Roskva. Her freckled face was red.

'You can't just be famous for doing nothing but squabbling and sashaying around in designer clothes!' Freya screamed. 'Do something. Earn our worship. Earn our devotion. Woden, you created our world. Save it. Save us.'

She stopped speaking, breathing hard.

'How dare you speak to your Gods like that,' said Woden. 'Get out of my sight before I kill you.'

'I've a mind to hurl you into Hel,' boomed Thor. The room shook. He gripped his hammer tightly.

'Get rid of her,' said the Goddess.

Freya put her hands on her hips. 'The frost giants are coming,' she said.

'I have a chat show to do,' said Woden.

'I have a film premiere,' said Thor.

'I'm doing my first *Vogue* cover,' said Freyja. 'So stop bothering us, Miss Doom and Gloom. Who says the frost giants are *actually* coming anyway? It could be a trick. Where's the proof? Now, Veronica, about my column in *ICE* this week, I could write about that first-night party, and the perfume launch . . .'

'Go,' murmured Roskva.

'We'll do what we can,' said Alfi.

Freya stomped out of the Archpriests Avenue mansion, slamming the massive front door behind her. She recoiled for a moment in the biting wind, then crunched across the semi-circular gravel driveway to the gatehouse, where the guard opened the electronic gates for her. She pushed through the fans and the photographers and journalists standing around in clumps outside the high fence. She looked for Snot but he was gone. One photographer half-raised his camera, and then lowered it when he realised she was nobody.

And now the world was ending. Meanwhile, her mum was out clubbing every night. Her dad was in Dubai. The Gods were partying and drunk on fame.

It's time to take matters into my own hands, thought Freya. If they won't do something, then I will.

Meanwhile

The golden-feathered rooster, who roused Woden's Valhalla warriors every dawn to start the day's battle, crowed a warning in the middle of the night. The startled warriors leapt from their pallets and snatched their bright weapons from the walls. The Gods trembled in their gleaming halls.

PART 4
THE FROST GIANTS

You Gods nourish your majesty
from the breath of prayer
and on dues of sacrifice,
and would be starving
were it not for beggars and fools.

Goethe, *Prometheus*

The Sleeping Army

Freya stood for a moment at the entrance to the British Museum, looking at the familiar stone steps and massive columns. She hadn't been back since that fateful night a lifetime ago. She found the thought of seeing the Lewis Chessmen, now that she knew who and what they really were, impossible to bear, especially as she'd come so close to joining their ranks.

She felt sick about blowing Heimdall's horn, about being blasted once again into the icy abyss. But she'd made up her mind. If the Gods were too deranged to take charge, then she would. A magical army of Woden's great warriors could fight giants, couldn't they? She tried not to think about her narrow escape from just one giant last time.

She climbed the stone staircase and entered room 40, the room dedicated to the Wodenic faith in the Middle Ages, the place where the Sleeping Army sat frozen on their chessboard, waiting to be woken. She paused for a moment, gathering her courage. It wasn't crowded: the hideous weather throttling Britain was keeping most people at home. There were two Japanese tourists, a whiny kid and his gran, and an elderly man dozing on a bench; otherwise the room was empty. The guard sat bored by the entrance, surreptitiously chewing gum.

The wood floor had been repaired, she noticed, the giant zig-zag crack filled in, all the fallen treasures rehung and the shattered exhibit cases replaced.

Averting her eyes, Freya walked slowly past the glass display containing the Lewis Chessmen. The ornate ivory horn, Heimdall's Horn, heavy with silver and glinting with jewels, was behind them, hanging mutely on its massive chains.

She was the Hornblower, and it was time to wake the Sleeping Army. Who knew what special powers they had, powers that could rout giants? Hadn't Woden enchanted them to sleep until a time of deadly peril? She hoped fervently she wouldn't have to lead them into battle, but she'd face that when it happened.

Freya swallowed and stood before the magnificent jewelled horn. She looked around to check if anyone was watching her, but the guard was sitting by the door staring into space.

Army, prepare to live again, she thought. Before she could falter she raised her lips to the narrow mouthpiece, bracing herself for the horn's thunderous roaring ringing, the icy whirlwind and her body ripping apart as she spilled into freezing space. Then she squeezed her eyes shut and blew.

Silence.

Huh?

Freya opened her eyes. All was as before, the guard staring blankly, the two Japanese tourists photographing one another in front of every artefact, the crabby child, the old man asleep on the bench.

I must have done it wrong, she thought.

She blew again, as hard as she could.

And again there was no sound. The guard suddenly turned to look at her. Freya reeled sharply away from the horn.

Feeling light-headed, her ears ringing in the silence, she walked over to the Lewis Chessmen.

The glass case was empty. The chessboard was still there, and the plinth, but the entire army had vanished.

Freya stifled a scream.

How had they escaped without shattering the case? Where were they? Why wasn't she with them? What had gone wrong?

There was a tiny white card inside the display. Freya read:

**THE LEWIS CHESSMEN
ARE CURRENTLY ON LOAN
TO THE CLOISTERS MUSEUM,
NEW YORK.**

On . . . loan? The Sleeping Army was on loan? *On loan?*

Why was she so unlucky?

'When are the chessmen back?' she gabbled to the guard.

The man yawned.

'The summer solstice, I think. Don't worry, we'll

get them returned safe and sound.'

'But we need them now,' wailed Freya. Everyone in the room stopped to stare at her. Even the smelly old man asleep on the bench woke.

Shivering, Freya walked back to the empty case and leaned her forehead against the cool glass. What now? She'd been all ready to sacrifice herself, and now this.

Why was her fate so hard?

She heard the sound of laboured breathing. The shrunken old man shuffled up to her, wearing several layers of mismatched, torn clothes and mumbling to himself. He smelled of grease and decay. Spittle collected on his chin. Freya moved away from him. Ugh. Gross. He looked like he was over 100 he was so wrinkled and decrepit. She didn't want to talk to anyone. Especially not now when she needed to think.

He tugged on her sleeve with his gnarled, spotted hands. His broken nails were filthy. Freya jerked away sharply.

'Looking for something, dearie?' he said, wheezing loudly. 'Perhaps I can help.' His breath was rank.

Freya shook her head firmly and walked away,

then pretended to be engrossed by the mosaic image of Woden displayed in the next Perspex case. Just leave me alone, she thought. I so don't need this.

The bent old man slowly sidled up beside her.

'Fate was with you last time, Freya,' he rasped. 'But no longer.'

She looked into his rheumy eyes, one red, one green.

Loki.

The Trickster God who had almost killed her. The Trickster God who had almost killed the Immortals. The shape-shifter. The Wolf's father. Loki the Liar and the father of monsters.

Freya choked. Her body jolted.

Run, she thought.

Loki gripped her wrist with surprising strength, then his hand weakened. She broke his shaky grip easily and pulled away, trembling and gasping. Should she scream? Could she scream?

'Not looking my best,' said Loki, coughing and leaning on the empty display case for support. His breathy, reedy voice crackled with age. 'Haven't been back to Asgard, obviously, so no apples of youth for me. I've become a sad, harmless, homeless old

God since we last met. Yeah, my daughter the corpse – thanks for asking, she's miserable as ever – she kicked me out. Can't say I blame her, but still, Hel isn't usually choosy about her guests.' He smiled. His few remaining teeth were cracked and black.

'Stay . . . away . . . from . . . me,' hissed Freya, trying to keep her voice steady. 'I'll tell the All-Father, he'll sort you out. Thor will put a hammer in your head. You monster.'

Loki waved his gnarled hand as if flicking away a fly.

'How about you buy me something to eat? I could murder a piece of chocolate cake. Great invention, chocolate.'

The Sly One leered at her with eager, sunken eyes.

'My brain is still working, you know. Not for much longer, so you'd better hurry up and decide. I just might be able to solve your little problem. Or – to be accurate – your giant problem. Heh heh, well, you gotta laugh, don't you?' he continued, then doubled over in an agonised fit of coughing. He was clearly struggling to breathe.

Freya hesitated as Loki gasped. Was this just a clever disguise? A trick to catch her off guard?

'Good girl. I knew I wouldn't regret not tearing you to pieces,' he rasped.

And somehow, without agreeing to anything, she was following him slowly downstairs to the great rotunda buffet café. Loki paused frequently to rest every few stairs.

There was some safety in a public place, thought Freya.

Loki piled up his tray with sandwiches, cakes and drinks. He slipped even more into his many pockets. Freya checked her purse. This would clean her out. Loki began stuffing his face with food even before she had paid. His hands shook so much she took the tray from him. His spilled drinks sloshed around the plastic.

They sat down at a wooden table beneath a banner advertising the forthcoming Viking exhibit. The other people at their table immediately got up and moved away.

Loki grinned a wolfish smile. 'I don't even notice my own stink any more,' he said, gobbling another sandwich. 'But then every man loves the smell of his own farts.'

Freya flinched.

'What are you doing here?' she hissed. 'You tried to kill me. You tried to kill all the Gods.'

Loki shrugged his sunken shoulders.

'It's true. I've been a bad boy. But I've learned my lesson. That was then. This is now.'

'You're the reason we're in this mess,' said Freya. 'You gave Idunn and her apples to the giants. You let the Gods get old.'

'I was unavoidably detained — Woden turned me into an ivory horse before I could rescue Idunn.'

'Liar. You stole Idunn from us,' spluttered Freya. 'You snatched her out of my hand.'

'Nonsense. I took her to Hel for safe-keeping. How could you be trusted with such a precious prize? I wanted to make sure all was well in Asgard before risking her return. What if the frost giants had invaded while the Gods were . . . indisposed?' said Loki. He drew his hand across his throat. 'Then *they'd* have the apples of youth.'

'That's ridiculous,' said Freya. 'The Gods wouldn't have been indisposed if you hadn't stolen Idunn in the first place. We almost died because of you.'

Loki made a rueful face.

'But you didn't. That was not your fate. And it

would not have mattered if it were. But let's focus on now. The frost giants are coming. You need me. Big time.'

Freya stared.

'Oh, you do. My father was a giant. I can talk to them. Make a truce. Bribe them to leave Midgard alone. They know I hate the Gods. Hated,' he corrected himself. 'They trust me. Meanwhile, I'll really be on your side. And the Gods'. A double agent.'

Freya laughed. 'Why should I trust you?'

Loki smiled at her with his strange eyes.

'You're right. Why should you? I could be a triple agent.' His mismatched eyes glistened for a moment. 'But look at me,' he said, coughing. 'I'm an old, old, drooling, stinking, arthritic, rheumatic, stumbling bone bag. The Gods have something I want: Idunn's apples. I've got something you need: my wiles. I'll help you beat the giants; you'll help me regain my immortality so I can return to Asgard. It's a win/win. Great expression, win/win.'

'What makes you think the Gods would take you back?'

Loki snorted.

'Oh, believe me it's much better to have me in Asgard pissing outside the walls than outside pissing in,' he said, wolfing down some brownies and gulping back a smoothie.

Freya flinched again. Was Loki really offering to help?

'It was you who tried to defame the Gods, wasn't it?' said Freya. 'All those malicious tweets and horrible stories . . .'

Loki looked sly. 'I had to eat,' he said. 'As you can see. Newspapers, websites – now that's a thing, a website – pay for gossip. When I think we relied on Woden's two ravens for all our news,' he added, shaking his head. 'And at the moment I am not getting any younger.' He wheezed a barking laugh. 'Quite the opposite in fact. I can't even turn myself into a fly. Great for eavesdropping, though, being a fly.'

Freya chewed on her sleeve. She could feel her brain whirring, straining to take all this in, trying to understand what he was – and was not – saying.

'You have Idunn's apples don't you,' said Loki suddenly. 'Oh, don't deny it, I saw you jump. And I'll bet you're being ever such a good girlie, guarding them, keeping them safe, giving their shiny golden skins a polish every now and then, and never ever being tempted to take a little bitty bite. But why shouldn't *you* be a goddess, Freya? Why shouldn't *you* be immortal? *You're* more heroic than they are. Bet they never even rewarded you for your services last time.'

Freya bit her lip and said nothing.

Loki looked at her shrewdly. 'Thought so. Those sons of mares. So typical. The Gods love you when they need you, and then – poof. *Hasta la vista* baby, and on to the next thing.'

Since when did a God say *hasta la vista*? thought Freya. Was this the weirdest conversation she'd ever had?

'Those ungrateful swines,' murmured Loki.

Loki was right, thought Freya. The Gods *were* ungrateful. They asked for everything, and gave . . . nothing. Well, not *nothing*, exactly. They'd given life, which, let's face it, was a big gift, but then it was take take take, do this, do that, worship us, sacrifice to us, obey us, praise us, honour us . . . or else. Wasn't it time the Gods gave *something* back? Or was it time for humans to look after themselves?

'Just imagine for a moment,' said Loki softly. 'You and me. Think what we could do together. Remake the world . . . haven't you always thought how good things would be . . . if *you* were in charge?'

'No,' lied Freya.

Who hadn't dreamed of ruling the world? She'd get rid of hunger, disease, war, beetroot and football. And her enemies, the whole mean girl clique.

Empress Freya. Freya the Immortal. Fabulous Freya.

'Of course, we can do this another way,' murmured Loki. 'Don't forget. I'm half giant. But so is my brother Woden. And Thor. The giants have had a terrible press. What makes you think they're so awful, anyway?'

'Because they're coming to kill us all?' said Freya. She shook her head to shake off her reverie.

Loki considered. 'Maybe you're no longer the Gods' biggest fan. Maybe they're unworthy of worship now. Maybe we need better gods. We could link up with the frost giants.'

'What?' said Freya.

'Just saying. No harm in saying. Once they've got rid of the Gods, you could rule down here, I could rule Asgard . . . all it would take is one little bite of an apple, Freya . . .'

Why was she listening to him? She knew *exactly* what happened when a mortal ate one of Idunn's apples. She'd probably regress to being a baby in nappies . . . forever. Like Clare, stuck in a teenage horror land.

Freya stood up.

'I've heard enough. Your mouth is full of lies.'

'Don't be stupid, Freya.'

'I'm going.'

'When you change your mind you can find me—' he screeched after her.

But Freya didn't wait to hear. She just wanted to get as far away from him and his weasel words as possible. She ran to the Tube, the harsh wind wet and raw on her face, through the eerily silent snow-smothered Russell Square Gardens. There were no squirrels. No pigeons. No sparrows.

The birds and animals had fled. There was only snow.

Meanwhile

Thor stopped dead doing his signature 'lightning bolt' gesture as he paraded around the bitter cold Arsenal football pitch after scoring yet another goal. Woden froze while signing autographs on a sleet-soaked red carpet. Freyja paused mid-sip at a champagne reception. Her feet in their six-inch-high gold Manolos wobbled, then she toppled over.

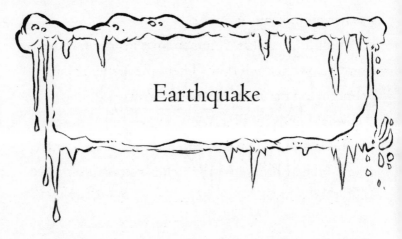

Earthquake

Freya jolted awake, shivering. What a horrible nightmare she was having. Then she realised it wasn't a nightmare.

What was that rumbling noise? It sounded like an explosion. Or an earthquake. There aren't earthquakes in Britain, she thought, as the house began to shake and her bed trembled violently. Every ornament on her chest of drawers oscillated back and forth, back and forth, a few shattering as they hit the floor. Her pictures swayed on the undulating walls as the air crackled around her and car alarms wailed up and down the road. All the street lights went out.

Freya's bed juddered to a halt as she clutched the quivering wooden headboard. Her breath came in gulps. What a time to be alone in the house. Where was her mum? Out. Always out.

A tumult of voices, commanding, insistent, came from below her window. Then the banging and pounding on her front door started up.

'Freya! Let us in! FREYA!!'

Oh Gods, it was Clare. She'd locked herself out again and had brought back a club-full of losers at 3 am. She tumbled down the stairs to the door.

'Mum, this is the THIRD time this week you've forgotten your keys,' she shouted through the front door. 'I think we've just had an earthquake.'

Freya undid the chain and opened the door. Gods and Goddesses pushed through. They looked wild-eyed and panicked as they streamed in, jabbering and clamouring.

'Where are they? Where is the All-Father? The frost giants have rampaged through Asgard!' they shouted as they packed into her house, spilling into the sitting room and running up and down the stairs.

Last time she'd seen them they were dying wraiths. Now they were young again, but frantic and frightened.

'Without Thor and Woden and Freyja we couldn't stop them,' said Njord.

'We've left 800 Valhalla warriors at the bottom of Bifrost,' panted Thor's wife, Sif. 'They will hold off the giants as long as they can.'

Last through the door was Heimdall, the watchman of the Gods. He carried the great ivory horn he must have ripped from the British Museum slung round his massive shoulders, the broken chains trailing and clanking behind him. In his right hand he clutched a red fire extinguisher.

'How did you—' began Freya.

'I stole my horn back from those thieves,' said Heimdall. 'Gjall is mine. What a load of old junk in that hoard. Cracked cauldrons and rusted swords and bits of old boat I wouldn't bury a dwarf in.'

'They're valuable because they're old,' said Freya.

'Bah,' snorted the God. 'Where's the gold? The silver? Though I did find this flame-quenching potion,' he said, brandishing the fire extinguisher. 'Now *that's* treasure.'

'Where are Woden and Thor?' shouted Njord. 'Where is the Goddess of Battle?'

'It's a long saga,' said Freya.

'Make it a short one,' said Tyr.

Our Gods

Freya's sitting room looked as if it was about to burst. Gods and Goddesses squashed onto the saggy sofa, perched on the sofa arms, and squished onto every chair in the house. Tyr and Njord sat glaring and cross-legged on the rug. Woden's handsome, armour-clad sons hunched by the doorway; Sif and Frigg and Bragi perched on the bay window sill; Idunn sat in her husband's lap; Heimdall skulked by the fireplace; Freyja's brother Frey slumped on the floor. Weapons cluttered the tables and leaned against the walls.

The front door banged shut. The Gods looked up. Freya saw the hope in their glinting eyes.

Clare strolled in, with mascara running down her face, her tights laddered, one broken-heeled shoe in her hand, and clutching a large bag of greasy chips. She was swaying slightly.

'Oh cool, a Viking costume party,' she giggled. 'Kinda boring, everyone just sitting around wearing old clobber. Come on, who wants to dance? Where's the beer?'

'Not now, Mum,' said Freya.

'Who is this mortal?' demanded Sif. Her lip curled.

'My mother,' said Freya, blushing.

'Your . . . mother?' said Frigg.

'This person dishonours us,' said Frey.

'Speak for yourself, weirdo,' said Clare. 'Have a chip.' And she danced in place, swaying to music only she could hear.

Should she confess? What did it matter now?

'She had a bit of an accident,' said Freya. 'With one of Idunn's apples.'

The Gods fell silent and stared at Clare. An angry hum filled the room.

Freya cringed. Would they kill her? Enslave them both?

'Wot?' said Clare. She continued munching.

Idunn, keeper of the apples of youth, went up

to Clare and touched her forehead with her cool fingers.

'Mum,' moaned Freya.

Clare shuddered. The chips dropped from her hand and spilled over the floor. She blinked rapidly, and her body trembled from head to toe. Her suddenly too tight mini skirt ripped.

'Mum?' said Freya tentatively.

'Freya,' mumbled Clare. 'I feel so dizzy.' She looked down at herself. 'Why am I dressed like this? Why is it so cold? Who are these . . .'

'Mum, no time to explain, these are our Gods, the frost giants are coming, we—'

'And I'm tattooed!' she shrieked. 'Freya, why do I have a snake tattoo on my wrist?'

'Mum, sit down and be quiet,' said Freya. 'Did you hear me? These are our Gods.'

Clare stared at the glowing Immortals. Their tall, bright, unearthly majesty filled the room.

'No,' she said. 'No . . . it can't be.'

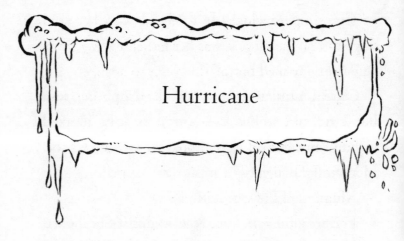

Hurricane

Clare, ashen-faced, her tense shoulders drawn up to her neck, kept to the edge of the room while the Gods argued, darting anxious glances at Freya every now and then. For once she looked completely out of her depth.

'Sorry there aren't enough chairs, my lords,' she said timidly. 'My hospitality is not what it should be. Crisps, anyone? Or I could send out for pizza,' she faltered.

'We will eat after we have fought and won,' said Njord. 'There will be feasting in Asgard.'

'Of course, of course,' said Clare. 'You keep out of this, Freya,' she added.

'I can't keep out of it,' said Freya. 'I'm already in it.'

Clare shot her a look.

Freya's phone rang. It was her father, calling from Dubai. She backed out of the room to answer.

'Uh, hi Dad,' she muttered. Bob's timing was always terrible.

'Freya, are you all right?' he said. 'I know it's the middle of the night—'

'No, I'm up,' she said.

'It's about the hurricane, I'm just checking to see you're okay.'

'What hurricane?' asked Freya.

'It's all over the news, turn on the TV,' said Bob. 'There's a category 10 hurricane heading straight for London. It's sprung out of nowhere. Wind speeds of 140 miles per hour and rising off the scale. The Home Office is urging everyone within the flood zone to move to higher ground or leave London. There's going to be massive flooding. The Thames is rising and going to burst its banks, and people are being evacuated and . . . Freya are you there?'

'Yes,' she said faintly.

'Freya, there's more . . .' Bob hesitated. 'There've been explosions at the Cloisters Museum in New

York, the chess pieces are missing . . .'

Freya gulped.

'Dad, this isn't a good time, we'll be careful, I promise.'

'Go to the top of the house,' he said. 'Get candles ready. Block up the front door with—'

The front door smashed down.

Freya screamed.

'Freya!' shouted Bob.

Thor burst in, then Roskva and Alfi. Gusts of wind rattled through the house. Freyja, Goddess of the Battle-Slain, followed, her hair wild.

'I'm here,' bellowed Thor, holding aloft his massive hammer in his iron gauntlet. 'Where are the giants?'

'You took your time,' snapped his wife, golden-haired Sif.

'What's that?' said Bob. 'It sounded like—'

'It's okay, Dad, gotta go,' said Freya, hanging up.

'My door,' said Clare, then turned to see Woden materialise in the middle of the sitting room in all his glory, wearing his gleaming golden helmet and brandishing the rune-laden spear which never missed and always returned to the hand that hurled it.

Clare went white. Then she bowed.

Woden ignored her.

'We heard Heimdall's horn,' said Woden. 'We are battle-ready.'

'Except I didn't blow it,' said Heimdall.

Freya opened her mouth and then closed it. Her phone rang again but she ignored it.

'The frost giants are heading for the rainbow bridge,' said Tyr. 'They'll be here by dawn. Without Thor's hammer and Woden's spear we weren't strong enough to hold them off in Asgard.'

Thor's face flushed. 'We've been busy here, you know,' he boomed. 'Noticed all the worship we're getting now? Look at you. The bright fame of the Gods is restored.'

'It seems to me it's been restored for a while,' said Njord.

'Shouldn't we call the airforce?' said Freya. 'The army?'

'To do what?' said Woden. 'Fight against storm and sleet and whirling winds? Because that is all mortals will see. This is a battle between Immortals. The tornado coming—'

'Why have you ignored us for so long?' said Clare suddenly. 'All these centuries, praying and

supplicating . . . and now you just turn up . . .'
Freya saw her hands shaking, as her mother
clutched the mantelpiece.

Woden frowned.

'Who are you to ask for attention from
the mighty Gods?' said Woden. 'Does the ant
burrowing in the ground demand *your* interest? Do
the salmon swimming in the river cry out that you
have forgotten them? We gave you life and that's
enough. Rejoice in that great gift. If anything we
were over-generous when—'

'Hush,' said Heimdall.

The Gods and Goddesses froze.

The Wind-shield of the Gods, who could hear
the grass growing, cocked his head.

'The frost giants are marching down Bifrost,' said
Heimdall.

'Take up your weapons and prepare for war,'
said Woden, grabbing his spear. His radiance
filled the room. 'The time of blood-wet spears is
upon us. Shields will be gashed. Shafts will sing
as arrows bite. Swords will clash under the battle-
storm.'

Freya began to slink from the room.

'Where do you think you're going?' demanded Woden. 'Put on your cloak of falcon feathers. We will need your eyes.'

Then Freya remembered. 'Loki is here,' she said. 'I saw him. He wants Idunn's apples.'

'Of course he's here,' said Woden. 'The Wolf's father is always around when there's trouble. Give me the eski. We don't want any more accidents.'

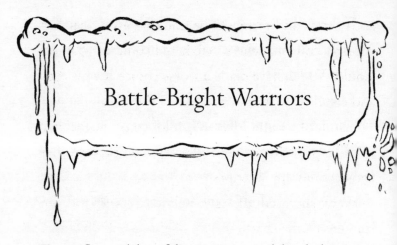

Battle-Bright Warriors

Freya flapped her falcon wings and landed on top of the high, hammer-shaped steeple of Woden's Temple. The biting wind blew fiercely and she had to grip tightly with her talons to keep her balance. Her juddering bird's heart pounded inside her feathery chest as her sharp falcon's eyes surveyed the hushed city below. The foggy, pre-dawn light was no obstacle: she could see for miles along the River Thames, then she turned to look past the London suburbs to the south, over the snowy hills of Surrey, glowing pinky-grey in the mist, across the meadows and fields and ancient woodlands of the Kent Downs all the way to the chalky cliffs of Dover and the choppy English Channel and beyond.

She shivered. What did she know of battles

and tactics and armies? She couldn't even beat her younger cousin at chess. She hated computer games. Could Woden have made a worse choice for his eyes and ears?

Just look, came Woden's cold voice inside her head, and I will see with your eyes. Where are my chosen ones, my warriors?

Freya surveyed the iron-helmeted ranks of the Einherjar, the battle-bright fighters of Valhalla, spread out in front of the Tate Modern around the base of the Millennium Bridge. They grasped their shining swords and axes, their spears and bows, their gleaming shields. Their red-gold coats of mail, flecked and battle-scarred, glinted in the swirling snow.

There's Snot, thought Freya.

Good, said Woden. We will need him.

Snot, grim-faced, wearing his filthy bear skin cloak, was at the head of a phalanx of berserkers on the north side of the bridge, clutching his battle-axe. Icy water drops dripped from the edge. Other warriors gripped their long spears, ready to rain down a shower of blood on the first giants to surge off Bifrost onto the bridge. In the still cold air the only sound in the empty city was the eerie clink-clank of armour as the warriors shifted from foot to foot, waiting. Waiting, in a thicket of spears. The murky Thames, studded with floating chunks of ice, slopped high against its banks, as if to escape the coming battle. Overnight, London had been hurled into the winter of winters.

What else? said Woden. What else?

Freya peered down at the silent fighters defending the narrow passage between the City of London School for Boys and the Asgard Army building. The London skyline of cranes and steeples, the Eye, Big Ben, Tower Bridge, the Gherkin, the Shard, the winding streets and gardens, all looked normal. Except, of course, for the surreal view of massed ranks of armour-clad warriors and the roads jammed with abandoned cars. Freya thought for a crazy moment of a film she'd seen, where warriors were superimposed on a blue screen ready for computer-generated images of orcs and elves to be added. The Gods were hidden . . . where? Freya had no idea. Would they spring out to fight? Or — and her heart went cold — had they fled, and abandoned them all to their hard fate?

'Look down, you stupid mare, we're in All-Father Square,' snapped Woden's voice. 'We want to take the giants by surprise. They think they will only be fighting mortals with their storms.' Freya saw the Gods, light-filled and blazing, spread out among the Sleeping Army. The chess pieces had heard her call and sprung back to life, the kings, queens, knights, rooks, pawns and their snorting horses, pawing the ground, steaming and shining.

Above them two ravens circled.

Surely the giants would be no match for the Gods, the Einherjar and the Sleeping Army. With Woden and Thor, how could—

The noise came first. A great whoosh of cloud and vapour. The bridge shuddered as hurricane winds whipped the Thames, which burst its banks in a tidal wave of ice-strewn water, spattering the shore and splashing the waiting warriors. Torrents of water flooded the streets, sweeping away all parked cars. The lights in the Shard and the Gherkin went out.

Freya saw Heimdall raise his horn to his lips. The ringing blast shattered every window for miles as the thunderous noise reverberated, rumbling and swelling, pealing and blaring.

The flaming rainbow road of the Immortals wobbled as it curved out of the dawn sky, hovering above the Millennium Bridge. Frost crackled across the railings, which snapped like brittle old bones and tumbled into the Thames.

Then the walkway buckled as the first giant lunged off Bifrost.

'They're here!' screeched Freya. The Valhalla warriors raised their shields, gripped their swords and charged.

The giant shook her swamp hair and hailstones fell from her lashes, punching holes in the metal bridge. Freya recoiled in horror. She looked as big as a building. Her hideous curved teeth stuck out from her mouth at crazy angles, like tombstones on a neglected grave mound. Spears of ice sprang from her hands like fingers.

'I am Iron Hag!' she roared. 'Prepare to die.'

More giants followed, dirt grey, with hair frozen into gnarled swirls of filthy snow. They bellowed their names: Hel Power. Whale-Head. Corpse-Eater. Blood Hair. Frost Lightning. Mouth Cramp. Horn-Claw. Spear Nose. Neck-Breaker. Lock-Jaw.

Jagged spikes burst from their shaking heads, like stalagmites. Half-gnawed seal carcasses tumbled from their matted hair and beards. Their eyes were like black pits with lava boiling behind them. They growled like the rumble of a glacier tearing and splintering into the sea.

Woden hurled his spear and a giant fell dead. His body shattered like smashed ice, then cracked into rubble, stones and gravel. Then the berserks hurled themselves at the giants pouring off the bridge as Thor's hammer crushed many of their skulls. Thunder cracked and boomed and lightning criss-crossed the exploding sky every time his hammer whirled.

'Go into the water and go under it,' Thor cursed them.

The bridge spun wildly, and broke. Freya heard the wrenching, tearing sound of bolts unbuckling as the bridge screamed beneath the giants' weight. A grating shriek; then TWANG TWANG TWANG as cables ripped and whipped into the massive bodies, hurling them off the madly swaying bridge. The water exploded around them as the river leapt its banks, burying the riverside buildings. .

The Valhalla warriors continued to charge at the never-ending stream of giants. Several fell through the churning ice and were swept away in the swollen current.

'DIE!' bellowed the giants, with the bottled rage of centuries.

The roaring giants loomed up everywhere, trailing clouds of frost and ice, stinking of dead fish, blotting out the sky. They heaved into view through the skyscrapers, towering over the Gherkin. Shards of ice fell from their bodies, freezing everything they touched, and the raging wind whirled chunks of ice into the sky. Freya's ears ached with the great CRUNCH STOMP of their pounding feet as they pulverised houses as if they were dead leaves and swung their arms to topple tower blocks, rip up lampposts and uproot trees, which they hurled at the Asgard warriors.

'The end is nigh,' shouted a man holding a placard in All-Father Square. A giant foot came down and squashed him.

Freya caught a flash of the Gods as they raced among the giants, slaughtering and hacking and hewing. And yet still the giants tumbled off Bifrost in an avalanche of fury and hatred. The berserkers charged at them, heedless, racing across the river using the rubble of the giants' bodies as a makeshift bridge.

Trees fell as the earth shook and shuddered. Buildings crashed down, lashed by the fury of the winds. Telephone wires tangled on the road, tripping the lumbering giants. The toppled electricity cables spat sparks as they dangled in puddles, hissing. Flood waters gushed through the narrow roads and poured through doorways.

'The power lines will electrocute you, be careful,' cried Freya.

'Electrocute?' said Woden.

'Fry you to a crisp,' said Freya. 'Don't fight them, keep away from them.'

One giant flattened the Globe theatre. Another wrenched the ten-storey chimney stack off the Tate Modern and swung it at Woden. The God ducked, and another giant was walloped in the face, falling into the river with an enormous splash before splintering into rocks. Whole sides of buildings collapsed as the grunting giants shoved them aside as if they were children's building blocks.

It's like the Blitz, thought Freya, as tower blocks gaped open, like overpacked suitcases splitting in flight. Except this time there were upturned cars balancing on roofs, and giants smashing through offices like slow-moving icebergs.

Thor picked up HMS *Wellington* and threw the boat into the swarm of giants storming down the Embankment. Several caught fire and exploded into flames as petrol poured down on them.

Freya saw the Gods for the first time in all their terrible power as they whirled amidst the venomous giants, slashing and destroying, smiting and hewing, figures of superhuman strength and speed amidst the howling wind and roaring flames. Thor hurled his hammer over and over, blinding the giants with flashes of lightning before the weapon shattered their skulls, cracking them into a thousand shards of ice and rocks before returning to his iron-gloved hand. Woden flung his lethal spear again and again. Panic and confusion reigned.

The frost giants fought back with hunks of masonry torn from buildings, and icicles sharp as daggers, but the nimble Gods were too quick.

And yet it seemed as if for every giant felled,

another two stepped forward, as more and more giants stumbled off Bifrost. The bodies of the Valhalla warriors lay everywhere.

Then Freya saw the Goddess of Battle, disguised as a large falcon, swooping amidst the giants and blinding them with her talons.

I could do that, thought Freya.

Stay put, mortal, ordered Woden.

As the hacking and hewing and carnage continued, Freya closed her eyes.

I can't bear to watch any longer, she thought, as an oozing giant extended his arm and sent several of the Einherjar flying into the Thames.

'Open your eyes!' commanded Woden. 'Tell me what you see.'

Freya forced herself to watch. Pretend it's a film, she told herself. Just describe a film. Pretend it isn't happening.

Freya saw giants scooping up cars and hurling them into the Valhalla warriors. The vehicles whirled through the air like Dinky Toys before landing with a sickening thunk. Freya's ears throbbed with the clang and hiss of weapons, the hideous thunder as Thor's hammer smashed skulls, the shrieking of trees splitting and rocks crashing.

A giant standing in the roaring Thames, the debris-strewn tide lapping his knees, looked straight at Freya. I'm a bird, she thought, curling into herself. Why should he notice me?

Suddenly the monster scooped up a cargo boat floating in the stormy river and hurled it at the dome of Woden's Temple. Freya flew off, but the mast caught her tail as the upturned boat landed on the steeple. Freya spun into the air, tumbled backwards, then plunged screeching into the midst of the battle raging in All-Father Square.

She lay there, stunned and winded, beneath a jumble of running legs while swords flashed above her. Then rough hands grabbed her.

'Get out of here before I kill you,' yelled Snot, flinging her back into the air.

Freya flapped her wings, then flew up and regained her high perch on the Temple, breathless and trembling, her shining feathers speckled with blood.

'Stop moaning – tell me where the leader is,' said Woden.

'Who?' said Freya.

'Thrym,' said Woden. 'The one who attacked you. Thrym.'

'He's breaking the Shard,' yelped Freya.

With a hideous howling yank, Thrym tore the Shard from its base. Then several giants carried it like a battering ram as they crashed their way through the City of London towards Trafalgar Square, wind and fire swirling round them, their hideous breath like a squalling cyclone.

Great dust clouds rose as the Gherkin disintegrated, blinding the fighters and obliterating her view. Woden screamed at her to tell him what she saw through the eruptions of dirt and metal and flying rubble. She flew about frantically, trying to catch a glimpse of the apocalypse taking place in Trafalgar Square below.

Freya twisted round and flew into a small patch of open sky to see Thor grabbing Cleopatra's Needle and bashing in a giant's mouth. The giant's chipped graveyard teeth sprayed out and clattered to the ground, like hail studded with nails.

'Take that, Iron Skull,' roared Thor.

Iron Skull snarled and grabbed Nelson's Column, which he swung at Thor and missed, knocking into the National Gallery instead, which crumpled into a heap.

Another giant yanked the London Eye off its axis and turned it into a Frisbee.

'Not this time, Grit-Teeth,' yelled Heimdall, catching it and whirling it back, slicing through Grit-Teeth's legs.

'Watch out, he's gnawing off the steeple behind you,' cried Freya, as other giants swatted at the Gods with the Fane's pointed tower.

The tide of battle swung back and forth. Sometimes it seemed the Gods were prevailing. Then the giants pushed back and the Gods and Valhalla army retreated, only to regroup and charge again.

With a terrible roar and a tearing of iron and sinew, Thrym and a host of giants ripped Big Ben off its foundations and hurled it at Thor. Thor fell to the ground and the missile flew over his head and crashed into Westminster Abbey.

'I've got Lock-Jaw,' yelled Woden, as a giant collapsed, howling.

'And I've killed Mud Bone,' whooped Thor, picking up the Shard which the giants had dropped and stabbing his prey, as Njord grabbed Nelson's

Column from the ground and whacked Spear Nose, who retaliated with a massive plane tree, which he jabbed at Njord until Thor rescued him.

Other giants scooped up the lion statues from their plinths in Trafalgar Square and threw them at the berserkers chasing them. A green-haired giant picked up a red double-decker bus and hurled it through Charing Hammer station, trying to stop the remaining Valhalla warriors from attacking. Freya gasped as she recognised Skadi, the hideous giantess whose father Freya had led to his death. Freya shrank inside herself, hoping that Skadi couldn't smell her.

And still the battle raged, on and on throughout that long storm-dark day. The remaining giants rampaged through St James's Park, trampling trees and uprooting bushes. The battle-weary Gods held them off in Green Park till the giants, roaring and snarling, retreated as the angry sky dimmed into darkness and the thumping, thudding battle sounds faded.

'Tomorrow we will destroy you!' bellowed Thrym. 'We will take over this land, seize the great gleaming halls, and command a host of followers.'

'Tomorrow *we* will destroy you!' bellowed Thor.

He gripped his bloody hammer in his huge bruised fist. 'Let every evil being have you.' His voice rang out across the dark, deserted, devastated city as night fell and the storm abated.

A Radiant Bride

Freya soared over the storm-battered, flooded, rubble-filled city. Flames rose from the fires raging along the Thames and throughout central London. The familiar skyline, with great holes ripped where Big Ben, the Shard and the Eye once stood was almost unrecognisable. Dead giants, crumpled to rock and boulders, littered the streets, along with uprooted trees, destroyed buildings and the twisted bodies of Woden's warriors. She watched, awestruck, as the Einherjar slowly rose from the dead, their bloody wounds healed, to regroup for the next day's battle.

Freya could see people huddled around campfires on Hampstead Heath, praying the hurricane would spare them, lighting candles at hastily erected altars, watching the battle-storm die out below. The wind had dropped, as if no hurricane had ever raged, but the freezing cold continued.

Suddenly, every fire was extinguished.

Woden must have used a fire-quenching charm, thought Freya. That's something at least.

'Freya, come to the Great Hall of the Priestess-Queen,' ordered Woden. 'Now.'

Freya wanted nothing more than to go home and sleep, but wearily she obeyed, turning back towards Green Park and Buckingham Palace.

Why, she thought. Why does he want me? But she was too tired to speculate further.

Down she swooped, over the black gates, into the Queen's great courtyard. The Gods and Goddesses emerged from the arches and shadows. Thor smashed down a door, and they entered the deserted palace.

Freya shook off her falcon skin and regained her human form. She was exhausted and hungry and cold. Her ears thrummed.

The shattered Gods gathered in the palatial red and gold throne room, the walls decorated with coats of arms and elaborate carved friezes. For once the Gods didn't look as if they'd been squeezed into a room and could stand up straight, the palace's gilt and embossed criss-crossed gold ceilings were so high.

The Immortals were cut and bruised, their faces smeared with grime, their bodies caked in mud and spattered with gore. Thor's clothes were torn and his massive fists were red and swollen. The Thunder God's mighty hammer Mjollnir dangled by his side, dripping oily blood onto the red carpet.

Only Woden glowed. His ravens sat on his shoulders, whispering in his ears, as he sat beside his wife Frigg on one of the two plush velvet thrones, facing the Gods who gathered below him in the vast gilt-decked room. Freya had never realised before how much the Priestess-Queen seemed to love gold, almost as much as the Gods, her immortal ancestors.

Idunn, Goddess of Youth, passed quietly among the Gods offering her golden apples. As they ate, their wounds healed. Roskva and Alfi scurried about dragging red and gold chairs into a semi-circle under the massive chandeliers, then took their accustomed places behind Thor. Snot, his grey wolf's bristle hair standing up, his matted bear skin rank and heavy with dried blood, glowered in the doorway. His gnarled arms gripped his venomous axe. Freya, uncertain, sat by Alfi and Roskva. Her stomach growled.

Woden stood and spoke.

'I am Woden, I am Oski, All-Father, Lord of Battle, Giver of Victory, and we are the Gods,' he intoned. 'Together we will free this world from the frost giants, so that people in Midgard can live according to the Commandments and Wisdom we gave them, united and—'

Yeah, yeah, thought Freya. Her appetite for this language had waned.

'. . . certain of victory, and our rightful place in—'

'Fine words you've unlocked from your word-hoard,' interrupted Woden's wife, Frigg. 'Save them for mortals. Who will be the first among us to say the truth?'

No one spoke. Woden glared at her.

'Then I must. We can't defeat them,' said Frigg. 'We barely held our own today. There are too many giants. We cannot overcome them. They cannot overcome us.'

There was silence as the Gods considered her fateful words.

'Frigg is right. We can fight them until neither

God nor giant is left standing, then we all lose,' said Njord.

The Gods looked at one another. Freya felt a flash of fear.

'Who will be first to ask for a truce?' said Sif.

'They will,' piped up a raspy voice behind Woden's throne.

Freya screamed.

There was Loki, tottering up on his withered legs from where he had concealed himself, clutching the throne to keep steady. He smiled at them.

'What's he doing here?' yelped Freya. 'He tried to kill me. He tried to kill all of you.'

Thor stood up, gripping his hammer. 'Get out of here, you rodent,' he bellowed, swinging his hammer over his head.

Loki yawned.

'Evening all,' he rasped. 'I bring a peace offer from the giants.'

The room exploded. Woden raised his hand. 'Let my blood brother speak.'

'Thank you, brother. But first I must rest my aching bones,' said Loki, stumbling down from the raised platform and jabbing Freya with his walking stick. She jumped up, scowling, and Loki sank into her chair.

'Though a sitting man soon forgets his tale, in my case there is no choice. An apple, Idunn, if you would be so kind—'

'No apples,' said Woden. 'Speak first, Sly One.'

Loki sighed and inclined his wrinkled, turkey-gobbler neck.

'But he can't be trusted,' Freya burst out.

'That was then,' said Loki. 'We're on the same side now.'

For how long? thought Freya. How could they trust him? He's so treacherous. So changeable.

'The Wolf's father is better in the fold than out,' said Woden.

'If One might be permitted a word in One's own home,' said the Queen, peeping her white head around the door, 'I should like to—'

Snot slammed the double doors in her face.

'Ohh,' gasped the Queen.

'Make yourself useful – bring us something to eat,' bellowed Thor.

'The frost giants are strong,' continued Loki. 'Brute strength cannot defeat them. They are regrouping for a final battle. This time they won't retreat until our bodies lie ripped apart. This quick world will freeze as they unleash their wind-cold ways, then they will seize our gleaming halls in Asgard. Imagine: giants ruling Asgard. Any Gods who survive will rot in exile.'

The Gods murmured.

'But there is another way. A crafty way. A wolf way to victory. Our enemies are strong, but slow-witted. I went to see Thrym, leader of the giants, and I bring a peace offer from him. The frost giants will leave Midgard.'

Freya's heart leapt. Could it be true?

'They will leave our bright citadel unstormed and return to their frozen lands. Asgard and Midgard will be saved.'

Hope returned to the Gods' pale faces. Roskva and Alfi clapped their hands.

'Sounds good to me,' said the Goddess Freyja. 'My nails are shot now. Do you have any idea how much a crushed black diamond manicure costs?'

'And in exchange?' said Woden.

'All Thrym asks is that we send Freyja to him as his bride.'

Freya thought she was going to faint.

'Me?' squeaked Freya. '*Me*! Marry a giant? Why . . .'

'Not you, herring face,' said Sif. '*Freyja*.'

For once, it wasn't her. Thank Gods and all the fates, it wasn't her.

The assembled Immortals gazed at the golden Goddess. Freya could see the calculation in their eyes.

For a moment she thought fire would pour from Freyja's mouth, as her body and throat swelled with fury. Her neck bulged and the links on her marvellous necklace burst apart, showering the throne room in a cascading clatter of tumbling, rolling jewels. The palace floor and walls shuddered with her rage.

'Not *another* giant who wants me,' shrieked Freyja. 'You can forget it. I'll never—'

'So if Freyja sacrifices herself for our good, as *I* did when I put my hand in the Wolf's mouth, then all is not lost?' interrupted Tyr.

'The frost giants would leave us and our bright halls alone?' said Heimdall.

'The world would not be wrecked?' said Frigg.

'And *all* we have to do is to give them my sister

Freyja?' said Frey. 'And we're safe? All-out war to the death is averted?'

Loki nodded.

'I say yes,' said Thor.

'Me too,' said Heimdall.

'I think it's a great offer,' said Frigg.

'If we don't, then giants will live in Asgard,' said Njord. 'Sorry, daughter,' he added.

The Goddess Freyja looked as if a bucket of scalding water had just been tossed over her.

'Are you all INSANE?' she screamed. 'Me, marry a *frost giant*? Me, marry an ogre? Me, marry a monster? I'd rather you all froze in Hel.'

'But Freyja, think about the greater good you would do,' said Njord. You would save the Gods. You would save the world of men. Your glorious fame would spread far and wide, and every—'

'Yes, my fame as an ogre-lover,' screeched Freyja. 'My fame as a floozy. My fame as an old tart.'

'I think we should send Thrym a radiant bride,' said Loki.

'*That*'s your great plan?' Freyja screamed. 'No way.'

Loki continued as if he hadn't heard.

'A well-swaddled bride. A timid bride covered

in heavy veils and long swishing skirts. A shy bride decked in the Necklace of the Brisings. A buxom bride with jangling keys at her waist and Thor's hammer Mjollnir hidden in her tunic . . . the hammer that cannot fail to hit its target, nor to return to the hand that hurled it, the hammer that can shrink small enough to be concealed inside a tunic or dangled from a waist with some jangling keys . . . I repeat myself,' said Loki. He frowned.

'I'm not listening to another word of this,' said the Goddess.

'Not you, cat-eyes,' said Loki. Then he paused. His face wrinkled. 'Where was I?' he muttered. 'I was thinking . . . thinking . . .'

'What is the Trickster on about?' said Njord.

Suddenly Freya understood.

'He means Thor should go disguised as Freyja,' she burst out. 'You know, like Achilles did, in the Greek myths, when he dressed as a girl to—'

'We have no interest in copying those dead sons of mares,' bellowed Thor, as everyone except him burst into howls of laughter.

Thor looked around the room at the hysterical Gods.

'Me?' bristled Thor. 'Dressed as a woman? Decked as a *bride*?'

'You'll look lovely,' said Loki. 'A nice flouncy cap, some rich brooches pinned just so, a long-sleeved tunic and a heavy veil. A VERY heavy veil. In fact, *several* heavy veils. I'll go with, disguised as his bridesmaid.'

'Loki, even swaddled in a thousand veils you are no one's idea of a bridesmaid,' said Heimdall. 'You're far too old and decrepit. You can barely lift your arm: how will you join battle with Thor?'

'I haven't agreed to this yet,' yelled Thor.

The Trickster's eyes gleamed.

'You can easily fix that. Give me an apple.'

Woden's eye narrowed. 'When and if the frost giants are defeated, you will be restored to youth and to Asgard. Till then you will remain as you are here. We need a warrior to attend Thor as his bridesmaid.' Woden surveyed the room. 'Snot can be the bridesmaid.'

Snot looked as if someone had just heaved a rock at his head. He growled, knotting his bristly grey brows together and baring his chipped black teeth.

'Roskva and Alfi will attend you both,'

continued Woden. 'Their youth will disarm the giants.' Freya saw Alfi go pale.

'I'm not shaving my beard and that's final,' bellowed the Thunderer.

'Loki, tell Thrym we accept,' said the All-Father. 'No,' he said, 'I prefer you where I can see you. I will send my ravens instead.'

He whispered in their ears, and the pair, Huginn and Muginn, flapped off.

The Gods and Goddesses, suddenly cheerful, huddled around Thor, swaddling him in long robes and heavy veils threaded with gold. Thor towered above them all, looking like an angry corpse as lace veil after lace veil hid his red-bearded face. Loki stretched out his withered legs on a pale blue silk sofa, directing the dressing. Snot's battle-scared head was also veiled, and his thick body draped in a richly embroidered, long-sleeved dress and shawl.

Freya tried not to smile, Snot looked so ridiculous. Hopefully, he would look the epitome of beauty to a giant.

'I'll kill anyone who *ever* speaks of this,' said Snot. He caught a glimpse of himself in one of the ornate mirrors and shuddered.

'Oh, just one more thing,' rasped Loki, coughing. 'So small I forgot to mention it. Skadi demands compensation for her father Thjazi's murder. She wants Freya.'

In the happy tumult of dressing the 'bride' and 'bridesmaid' Loki's fatal words barely rippled.

Freya went cold.

'Me?' squeaked Freya. 'Or the Goddess?'

Loki fixed her with his fathomless eyes.

'Skadi is thirsting for vengeance against *you*, mortal, for her father Thjazi's murder,' said Loki. 'As is her right.'

'But I didn't kill him,' said Freya. Her heart squeezed. Skadi. Thjazi. Two names she'd hoped never ever to hear again.

'You led him to his fiery death in Asgard,' said Woden.

'At your command,' said Freya. If her heart beat any louder it would echo around the room.

'A leader has been killed, and compensation must be paid,' said Woden.

'Can't you give her gold?' begged Freya. Gods know, they had enough of the stuff.

Thor laughed. 'You saw Skadi's storm-home.

It is filled with gold.'

'Only you will satisfy her,' said Loki, yawning.

Why could she never escape her entanglement with the Gods? Just when she thought she was free, they'd yank her back on her chain, a pawn in a cosmic game she would never understand.

Alfi squeezed her hand. 'I'm sorry,' he whispered.

Roskva refused to look at her. Why should she, when her own grim fate was almost as bad?

'But . . . what will she do to me?' quaked Freya. 'What does she want with me?' She well remembered Skadi's angry face, her tree-trunk legs, her disgusting smell. Use her as a pillow? Keep her as a slave in Thrymheim, her cold dark storm-home, gutting fish for eternity? Hurl her over the cliff?

'That is not our concern,' said Njord. 'She is owed compensation and she has demanded you. A very modest request. We want to end the blood feud with her race.'

Freya looked pleadingly at the other Gods, while they primped and attached richly jewelled brooches onto Thor's white overdress.

'Oy! Watch how you pin that,' he snapped.

'Looking good,' said Frigg.

'You should rejoice to have this chance to serve us,' said Heimdall, pinning a three-lobed brooch at Thor's neck and standing back to consider the effect. 'Perfect.'

'Rejoice?' said Freya.

'Life is harsh and unfair,' said Woden. 'Even we cannot escape our fate. Now let us move on to more important matters. Where should we be while Thor is hammering the giants?'

'Please let me call my mum,' said Freya.

'Shhh!' scolded Tyr. 'The Lord of the Gallows is speaking.'

'Be quick,' said Woden, as the Gods continued in their Council.

Hands shaking, Freya punched the speed dial on her phone and moved away from the Gods towards the door. As usual, her battery was almost dead. Clare answered instantly.

'Freya. Thank the Gods. I've been so worried. Where are you? I've been calling and calling but the phone lines are down. Tell me you're nowhere near the hurricane. Are you all right?'

Freya gulped.

'Fine. Fine. Mum, I have to go . . . go on a journey.'

She could hear her mother's antennae twitch.

'Journey? With . . . them? Where?' said Clare sharply.

'Just . . .' Freya fell silent. Stratford, and then Jotunheim, the land of the giants? Her mouth was cardboard. 'Just a journey. But I'll be fine, Mum, really.' Freya struggled to keep her voice even. What was the point of alarming her?

Roskva gestured angrily. 'Hurry up,' she muttered. 'Time won't wait.'

'Gotta go, Mum.' She wanted to add, 'I love you,' but she couldn't say the words.

'Freya! Don't—'

'Bye.' She clicked off her phone.

If she couldn't avoid her fate, she would try to face it bravely. That much she had learned. Her only hope was that Thor would kill Skadi in the battle to come.

'My ravens tell me the giants are camped in the great stadium of games encircled by the river, east of here,' said Woden. 'The one mortals call the Olympic Stadium.'

'How will we get there?' said Freya. 'We can't exactly hop on a bus or take the Tube.' Would they make her walk towards her hard fate?

'You will ride in Thor's goat chariot,' said Frigg. 'The Einherjar have brought it here.'

Of course they have, thought Freya bitterly, as she followed the others out of the throne room.

The Horse Might Talk

Thor and Snot trudged down the curved gold stairway, clutching the banister and trying not to trip over their dragging skirts. They passed the Queen on the stairs, carrying a tray of sandwiches and pies. Thor snatched a handful as he descended.

The Gods gathered in the frosty courtyard to see the bridal party off. Someone had already opened the black iron gates. Above them, on the palace first floor, a curtain twitched and a crown peeked out.

The goats reared and stamped as they stood in their halters, glistening in the freezing night air, their fur flecked with snow, eager to start.

Freya knew all about Thor's magic goats, which could be eaten and yet spring back to life so long as their intact bones were thrown onto their skins.

These were the ones that had caused Roskva and Alfi to be enslaved long ago, when Alfi had disobeyed Thor and gnawed on a leg bone. Freya, teeth chattering, felt like she was falling into a feverish dream.

Snot stomped over to the waiting chariot. He kept forgetting to hitch up his long skirts, and he stumbled on the gravel. The clomp of his heavy footsteps carried through the stillness.

'Snot, don't stomp,' hissed Roskva. 'You're a bridesmaid.'

'This is how I walk,' bellowed Snot.

'And no bellowing,' snapped Roskva. 'Master, that goes for you too. You're the goddess Freyja. She doesn't bellow – well actually she does sometimes, but – you know what I mean. Just keep saying to yourself, 'I'm a Goddess. I'm a Goddess. I'm the loveliest Goddess in all the nine worlds.'

The veiled Thor turned to look at her. His eyes blazed through the heavy fabric.

'Say that one more time to me and I'll kill you,' he roared.

'Unless I kill her first,' growled Snot.

'I'm only trying to help,' said Roskva.

'Get in and be quiet,' said Thor, as he followed Snot into the fur-lined chariot and grabbed the reins. Roskva, Alfi and Freya climbed in and sat behind him, covering themselves in bear skins.

To Freya's surprise, all five of them fitted comfortably inside. Her eyes darted about. Could she jump from the chariot and flee for her life? Yet if it was so fated she should be handed to Skadi, her harsh fate would catch up with her wherever she was.

'Follow the river to the giants,' said Woden. He whispered to Thor, who nodded, then yelled at the goats who immediately galloped off into the black night.

The goats hurtled down the foggy Mall through the darkness of Green Park, now flattened and devastated. A few faint stars glittered above them. The air smelled of fire. The chariot jolted as the goats wove through the fallen trees and rocks without breaking stride. Freya clutched the side, praying they wouldn't crash. Alfi squeezed her freezing hand. 'It's okay, the goats never stumble,' he whispered. His breath floated like puffs of smoke around his face. 'And don't despair.'

'We must all do as destiny decides,' said Roskva. 'Fate is remorseless and holds dominion over us all. And don't I know it.'

'Once I was taken prisoner by a King and sentenced to death,' said Snot. 'And I told him if he spared my life for one year, I would teach his favourite horse to talk. The King agreed. Everyone mocked me. You can't teach a horse to talk, they said.

'A lot can happen in a year, I replied. The King might die. I might die. Or the horse might talk.'

'What happened?' said Freya. She'd never heard Snot speak so many words.

Snot shrugged. 'As you see, I am still here.'

Despite herself, Freya smiled.

The jerking chariot moved swiftly along the deserted roads, splashing through puddles and flood water, somehow gliding over the rubble from the great battle, following the river towards the Olympic Stadium where the giants waited.

'Master, remember to toss your head the way Freyja does,' said Roskva. 'Don't forget you've got golden curls beneath your cap.'

'I will not toss my head,' said Thor. 'Isn't it enough I'm swaddled in a bridal veil and dress? Wearing a necklace so heavy it would choke an ox? And a frilly cap?'

'I swear by the Gods,' said Snot, 'if I'd known I'd be falling on my face getting my feet twisted up in skirts I'd rather have been left for dead on Hekla.'

They fell silent the closer they got to the stadium, which loomed up in the darkness, encircled by freezing fog, the iron air dense and malevolent. Freya heard the whirling winds roaring inside the arena, as if a ferocious tempest had been bottled within its walls. Hail, sleet and snow blasted them. The Olympic Stadium had become a reeking storm-house for frost giants.

Freya could hear their raspy voices filling the night, like the terrifying whoosh of hurricane winds. Flaming torches had been set all round the arena's high circle, where the 5012 Olympics had been held. Now hideous frost giants patrolled the perimeter, their stumbling, lumbering bodies shadowy boulders against the eerie night sky. The monsters who had come to destroy her world had made themselves at home.

Freya trembled as the goats juddered to a halt beneath the twisted red steel observation tower outside the howling stadium. Her final moments of freedom before she was handed over to Skadi.

Freya's legs felt like rubber. She cowered under the bear skins. If only she could she'd stay here forever, comforted by the enveloping warmth of the furs, just to snuggle down and—

Snot pushed her out of the chariot.

'You've got legs, haven't you?' he snarled. 'Why is it that every time I'm with you something awful happens to me?'

'I could say exactly the same thing about you,' said Freya.

'Quiet, both of you,' said Roskva. She glared at Freya. 'Master. Snot. Please. If you must speak, talk in high-pitched voices only. Otherwise you'll give yourselves away and we'll all die.'

Thor grunted.

Snot growled.

Freya despaired. Were these two the least likely women ever? How could Midgard's survival depend upon Thor of all the Gods persuading Thrym that he was the loveliest Goddess in the world? Freya turned and took her last look at London.

Whatever happened she was already lost.

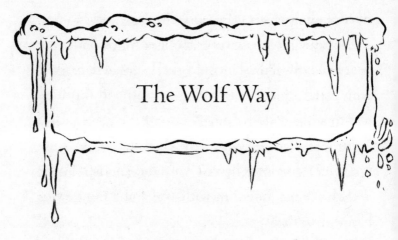

The Wolf Way

The bride, her bridesmaid, and their three mortal attendants walked slowly through the entranceway into the tumultuous, creaking stadium, the high oval walls barely containing the surging storm raging within. Thor and Snot struggled to keep their long skirts from flying up over their heads as the icy, roaring winds pelted them with sleet. Freya would have been swept off her feet in the lashing winds if Snot hadn't grabbed her arm.

'How do you walk in these horrible flapping things?' grunted Snot. 'If I find the person who invented skirts I swear by the Gods I'll kill them.'

Freya paused, teeth chattering, at the entrance to the great stadium. Where athletes had performed deeds of wonder on the orange track before thousands of screaming spectators, now the arena was packed with sprawling giants and massive, billowing tents. It was like walking into a giant refrigerator filled with rotting food.

A terrible voice boomed out over the vastness like hailstones clattering onto steel, then an immense block of ice loomed up out of the stormy blackness.

'She's here! My Freyja has come. The fairest Goddess of all is mine!' The ground shook as Thrym shambled up to them, leading the way to the enormous tent pitched over the entire middle of the stadium, bellowing commands as he lumbered.

'Black Tooth, lay on the wedding feast! My bride is here. Lead her to the High Seat. Mouth Cramp, bring mead horns. Iron Hag, see that my bride has everything she needs. Skull-Splitter! Gravel Yeller! Evil Thorn! Everyone, come. Come. Freyja is mine!'

'Remember, both of you, no stomping,' hissed Roskva. 'Our lives depend upon it. Think dainty. Dainty.'

Freya, Roskva and Alfi trailed behind the sturdy bride and her stout attendant as they entered Thrym's tent. Small lights flickered around the sides, but the place was dark and shadowy. Straw covered the ground and the benches, and bones crunched beneath their feet. Freya gagged. The rank air smelled like the place where seals go to die.

'This way, this way, my petal,' boomed the King of the Giants. He gripped Thor and gave him a huge slap on the rump. Thor growled.

'My, my, what a fine filly Freyja is,' bellowed Thrym. 'I like a girl with meat on her bones. Sit in the High Seat beside me, Freyja,' ordered the giant, grinning his fishy grin.

The veiled bride flung himself into the chair of honour beside Thrym, about as gracefully as a whale. Thor's bridesmaid, Snot, squeezed in beside him. Huge as Thor was, Thrym towered above him. Roskva and Alfi stood watchfully behind Thor, and Freya huddled beside them. Her teeth chattered uncontrollably. It was like standing inside a freezer. Thank the Gods, the place was dimly lit, which would help Thor's disguise.

The giants who'd followed them inside the enormous tent immediately sat drooling at the vast table. She looked for Skadi, but couldn't see her. She was lurking somewhere, Freya was sure, waiting to pounce.

Freya ducked behind Thor's high chair and tried to keep out of view. If any of these monsters trod on her she would be squished instantly. She shivered. When would she be grabbed and handed over to Skadi? The giants lumbered about, stinking and slobbering. The noise of guttural voices, raised in drunken victory, billowed through the tent. The drunker they became, the more they drank, spilling mead which flowed unceasingly.

The long trestle table was piled with vast platters of frost-covered food: oxen, seals, venison, and dozens of salmon. Horns of mead were scattered the length of the huge table.

Freya forced herself to look at Thrym. His filthy hair and beard were caked with swamp grass and dirt and ice. Bristly tufts sprouted all over his face. His foul breath wilted everything it touched. His greasy hands and knobbly arms were covered in warts, and pus-filled lumps dotted his bull neck. His thick tongue wetted his blubbery mouth.

'And who is my Freyja's charming bridesmaid?' boomed the giant.

'Snot,' came a deep croak beneath the veil.

Roskva and Alfi went white.

Aaaarrghh! Snot had given them all away, thought Freya. She gripped the back of Thor's chair.

But Thrym didn't seem to notice.

Freya breathed again.

'Snot. A beautiful name for a beautiful bridesmaid,' said Thrym.

What good fate that Snot's parents had given him a girl's name, thought Freya.

'What an alluring low voice she has,' said Thrym.

'Her voice croaks from singing songs of joy for her mistress,' said Roskva quickly.

'And is Freyja's voice just as delicious?' asked Thrym, poking his bride in the ribs.

'Freyja has taken a vow of silence until the happy moment when she becomes your wife,' said Roskva.

Thrym belched.

'What delicacy! What elegance!'

Roskva was a grump, but she did have quick wits, thought Freya.

'Grit-Teeth! Whale-Head!' bellowed Thrym. 'Bring in the plate of dainties for my Goddess and her bridesmaid.'

Two giants stumbled in carrying a platter with some small roasted birds and a few berries and placed them before Thor and Snot.

Thor scooped up and ate the 'dainties' in one mouthful, then snatched a mead horn and downed it in one gulp, then a second, and a third. Next he shovelled a salmon under his veil into his mouth, then another, and another, swallowing each one in a few chomps, followed by half an ox.

Thrym stared at his bride with his flaming eyes, his pustulant mouth drooping open, his grisly fangs covered in gristle.

'She can really stuff it in,' said Thrym, licking his bulbous white lips. 'I've never seen a woman eat and drink so much.'

Oh Gods. They were rumbled.

'Freyja hasn't eaten in ages,' twittered Roskva. 'She was too excited about her wedding night.'

Thrym grinned, showing off his rusty spiked teeth.

'I like a woman with a healthy appetite,' said Thrym, walloping his bride on the back. Thor fell off his seat face forward into his salmon the blow was so powerful and unexpected. Freya saw him clench his fist around his hidden hammer as he righted himself, chunks of salmon clinging to his veil. Roskva brushed it off as best she could.

'. . . and with some meat on her bones. Ha! No scarecrows for me,' said Thrym, the icy air filled with his foul breath. The other giants continued stuffing food into their lumpish mouths, their frozen beards filling with meat and grease. They drank horn after horn of mead, roaring louder and louder the drunker they got. Several had passed out and were snoring on the table, their heads buried in bones and fish heads.

'Please, just a little kiss, my petal,' boomed Thrym, smacking his rubbery lips and reaching out to lift Thor's veils with his massive, frost-bitten fingers.

'NO!' said Roskva. 'Not until you're married. Woden forbids it. It is not our custom for you to see your bride before you're wed. This is the Goddess Freyja, not some troll. Stand back.'

'Then let's have the wedding NOW!' roared the giant. 'I can't wait to kiss my bride and admire her peerless beauty.' He leaned closer to Thor's face. 'Jus a lil' peek . . .' he slurred, then he started back as if he'd seen a monster.

'Why are Freyja's eyes like burning coals? Never have I seen eyes so fierce.'

'What do you expect, Lord?' said Roskva. 'She

hasn't slept for many nights, hoping that one day you'd ask to marry her.'

The giant roared his approval and whacked Thor on the back again. Thor spat out his drink all over the table.

'Not long now,' Thrym roared, leering at her. The few frost giants who weren't hopelessly drunk joined in, pounding the table, shouting, 'Now! Now! Now!'

'We'll leave right aw—'

Thor whipped off his veils, leapt to his feet and sent his hammer hurling at Thrym, crushing his skull, then launched his fearsome weapon straight at the row of drunken giants. 'My hammer will shut your mouths!' he bellowed, as Snot ripped off his skirts, pulled out his axe and sword and attacked.

Roskva and Alfi hurled plate after plate of food at the befuddled giants. Freya, uncertain, threw a frozen salmon, then dived under the High Seat. Roskva and Alfi did the same as above them was the whizz and crack of bones, the grunting and howling and shrieking and thudding as bodies fell and benches overturned and the tent's walls ripped and collapsed as fleeing giants trampled through them. And again and again she heard the whizz thud smash of Thor's hammer as it found its target and returned to the Thunder God to be re-launched.

Hidden from the battle, the three clutched one another. Freya prayed as she had never prayed before.

There was shouting outside the tent and the sound of stamping feet. More giants. She'd thought they'd all been at the feast. Who were these newcomers? Now they'd all be killed.

Freya opened her eyes. Through the bench legs she saw the pounding legs of the army of Valhalla warriors hacking and hewing their way through the remaining frost giants, who crumbled into rubble as they tried to flee.

'Stop them!' came Woden's unmistakable voice.

'You took your time,' grunted Thor, his hammer whizzing and thunking around the tent.

And then, finally, there was silence. No wind. No screams. No thuds. Just silence.

Stunned, Freya, Roskva and Alfi climbed from their hiding place. What remained of the tent was littered with bloody, melting blocks of ice, boulders, rubble, and rocky fragments, while the victorious Gods and Einherjar roamed over the blood-fouled, fuming earth, snatching gold armbands and fine swords.

Something was different. Freya sniffed. The wintry storms had gone. The sulphurous air had passed into spring mildness. Dawn sunlight streamed through the clouds in bright streaks of tangerine, gold and pink while early morning mist rose from the boulders and slippery rocks strewing the stadium.

The Gods whooped and cheered. The Valhalla army bellowed and clashed their swords on their shields. The Lewis Chessmen stomped and yelled. Roskva and Alfi beamed at one another. Was she free? thought Freya. Had Skadi been killed? Could she dare to hope that it was not fated that she—

Suddenly Heimdall stiffened.

'A giantess approaches,' he shouted.

At the top of the stands, a helmeted warrior stood in a coat of chain mail, clutching a golden shield and holding aloft a sword and spear. The rising sun lit up the weapons, spiking dazzling rays of light around her like Valkyrie's wings.

'I have sworn vengeance on my father Thjazi's murderers,' she roared. 'I demand compensation to end my feud with the Gods.'

Freya's heart tightened. It was Skadi. She had rejoiced too soon.

Skadi, squeezed into her armour and with a helmet perched tightly upon her tangled, frizzy green hair, stomped down from the top of the spectator stands to ground level where the Gods gathered. When she reached the bottom she threw aside her round shield, covered in red-beaked eagles with gold eyes, gnawing at a corpse. Freya recoiled. The same hideous warty face. The same, terrible squinting bloodshot eyes. The same long, curved, filthy nails. The same horrible dead fish stench. Skadi. Was there any creature alive who hated her more?

Thor raised his hammer.

Woden shook his head. 'No,' he said. 'Enough blood has been shed. We wish to be at peace now. Skadi comes for her rightful compensation.'

Freya's throat was dry. There would be no victory celebrations for her.

'I made my terms clear,' said Skadi. 'Where is my handsome husband?'

Freya jumped.

'Husband?' said Woden.

Skadi looked at the shuffling Gods. Her gaze fixed on Snot.

She looked more closely at him and laughed her horrible laugh of screeching tyres. 'Surely you weren't thinking that bear-breath berserker was a fit husband for *me*, Skadi, daughter of Thjazi, King of Giants?'

'Say that again and I'll kill you,' growled Snot under his breath.

'And what's *she* doing here?' Skadi pointed at Freya.

'The Gods brought me as your compensation,' said Freya, shaking. She struggled to keep her voice steady.

'You? Why would I want *you*, you little thief,' said Skadi.

'Loki said you wanted . . . me in compensation for your father's death.'

'You? What kind of lousy reparation would that be, for the death of a king!' screamed Skadi. 'You? You?! A scrawny, whiny mortal like you? For what, fishing bait? To clean my snow shoes? What good would that do? Why in Hel's name would I want you? Once I'd squished you, or hooked you for bait, where would I be?'

Freya felt as if a tiny bit of blue sky had suddenly emerged from the smothering clouds.

Was it possible that . . .

'The Trickster said you wanted me,' whispered Freya.

'NO!' howled Skadi. 'I want PROPER compensation for my father's death.'

So Loki had lied. Why wasn't she surprised?

Roskva and Alfi gripped her tightly. Freya feared if they hadn't she would have fainted. Relief flooded her.

'What do you want then?' asked Woden. 'Gold?'

'No,' said Skadi. She spat. 'I have mounds of gold and piles of jewels. I have so much gold I could cover Thrymheim ten times over and still have storerooms bursting with gems. No gold.'

'Then what will you take?'

'I want a husband. It's lonely in my beautiful ice palace. My storm-home echoes with loneliness.'

The Gods murmured quietly among themselves.

Then Woden spoke:

'The feud between Gods and giants must end. Skadi has a right to compensation. You may choose your husband from among us, but only by his feet,' said Woden.

Skadi looked startled.

'His feet?' said Skadi. 'Why his feet? Couldn't I see his—'

'Because that is my decree,' said Woden. 'Do you want a husband or don't you?'

'I do,' said Skadi. 'Oh, I do.' She looked at the handsome Frey, and winked.

Frey didn't wink back. He actually looked a little green.

Frey is probably hoping his feet have cracked nails and bunions, thought Freya.

Skadi turned her back as the Gods assembled in a row, removing their boots and shielding their faces with their tunics.

'We're ready,' said Woden.

Skadi moved slowly along the line, peering at the Gods' feet.

She stopped in front of one, moved on, then slowly returned.

'I choose . . . him,' said Skadi.

The chosen God put down his tunic. It was Njord, Lord of Seafarers and Sea Creatures, with his weathered skin, and sea-salt smell.

Freya saw him gulp as he looked into the red eyes of his bride.

Skadi stepped back and grimaced.

'I've been tricked,' said Skadi. 'I wanted—'

'You could have been given Loki, so rejoice in whom the fates have chosen for you,' said Woden. 'A fair reward for your father's death, and the death of all the frost giants. In fact, you have got the better bargain.'

Skadi and her husband-to-be exchanged grimaces.

'We're living in the mountains,' scowled Skadi. 'I hate the sea.'

'We're living by the seaside,' scowled Njord. 'I hate the mountains.'

'You can spend nine nights in each,' said Woden sharply. 'But before you go, I have one more gift for Skadi, to mark the end of our enmity.' Reaching into his tunic, the All-Father removed two enormous liquid marbles.

'Those are my father's eyes,' said Skadi.

'Watch,' said Woden, and he hurled the eyes high into the heavens.

'His eyes are twin stars now,' said Woden, 'and

for so long as this quick world lasts, they will look down upon you, and upon all of us.'

Skadi gazed into the sky. Then she nodded, and picked up her weapons. Njord, his face white, followed her.

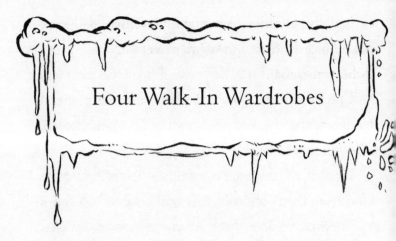

Four Walk-In Wardrobes

'Poor Dad,' said Freyja, applying lipstick to her bee-stung lips.

'Rather him than me,' said Heimdall.

'That was a close call,' said Tyr.

'You're telling me,' said Woden's handsome son, Vali. His brother Vidar laughed.

'It's time we went back to Asgard,' said Woden. 'We don't belong here any more.'

'I'm not going back with you,' said Freyja.

'What do you mean, you're not going back?' said Woden. 'Our time here has ended.'

'I'm staying in Midgard,' said Freyja.

'You *choose* to live with the sons of men?' said Sif. 'Instead of the heaven of Asgard?'

Freyja tossed her head. Was it Freya's imagination,

or had the Goddess put highlights into her glossy gold hair? It had a distinctly metallic hue Freya didn't remember.

The Goddess opened her mother-of-pearl compact, and checked her bright red lipstick. Stolen, I bet, thought Freya.

'First of all, there are no shops in Asgard,' said the Goddess. 'I was always wearing the same old robes and necklace. Here there are thousands of dresses, millions of jewels. And the shoes! It's worth staying just for the shoes. What's there to do in Asgard, except drink and fight and spy on humans? Nothing. Nada. Zilch. Whereas down here . . . I've never had so much fun.'

'But you always said how much humans smell,' said Frigg.

Freyja shrugged. 'I've got used to their stinkiness.'

'And the noise? You never stopped complaining,' said Thor.

'No noisier than all those spears and shields clashing every day, and all those drunken warriors yowling every night.'

'And what about your beautiful hall, Sessrumnir?' said Sif.

'Puh!' said Freyja. 'That old hovel? It's draughty. It's cold. It's just a big old lump of gold and stone. Did you know I've got four walk-in wardrobes in my mansion here? Central heating. An indoor gym. A swimming pool. No more dips in those icy rivers for me. I don't know how I put up with it for all those centuries. I'm a style icon. I'm worshipped. My picture is in every magazine. Now if you'll excuse me I've got a manicure and massage booked for this afternoon. I'm being interviewed later this week for *Home Beautiful*. Then I'm being photographed for *Vogue* – Freyja: Goddess for Our Time is the headline.'

'And what about your husband, Od?' said Woden coldly. 'And your daughter Hnoss?'

Freyja rolled her eyes. 'Oh, *them*. I'll drop by Asgard from time to time, don't you worry, see how you're all getting on, pick up one of Idunn's apples . . .' And off she clattered on her high-heeled, crystal-encrusted shoes, barking into her diamond-covered mobile and swinging her enormous Gucci leather handbag.

'Let her go,' said Woden. 'She'll come to her senses. Soon she will be old news, and other goddesses will replace her. As one day, we will be replaced. I know that now.'

'All the more reason to live for today,' said Loki, tottering over to them, as old and decrepit as ever. 'Give me the apple I have earned.'

Woden nodded, and Idunn handed a golden apple to the Trickster. He gnawed at it frantically with his few remaining teeth. Freya turned away. She didn't want to be near him when he regained his youth and strength.

'I'm going home,' she said. She felt in her pocket for her falcon feather. One last flight, she thought. One last flight.

The Gods and Goddesses, watching Loki intently, ignored her.

Roskva and Alfi were busy with Thor's chariot, making it ready.

'Till next time,' said Alfi. 'When it is so fated we meet again.'

'There's bound to be a next time,' said Roskva. 'Unfortunately.'

Alfi scooped up a jagged piece of steel grey rock and gave it to her.

'Here,' he said. 'A remembrance of a great battle

you alone in Midgard witnessed.'

Freya shook her head, shuddering. A piece of a giant's body? No thanks.

'Maybe you could come for a visit one day?' she said. 'And we could just do some normal stuff — hang out, see a movie, go shopping . . .' Her voice trailed off.

'Be lucky,' said Alfi.

'Be fortunate,' said Roskva.

'Be blessed,' said Freya.

The brother and sister linked arms as they walked back to Thor.

Woden's voice drifted through her head as she shook out the falcon skin.

'Mortal,' he said. 'May you enjoy a longer destiny. Act in a way which will be long remembered when life is over.'

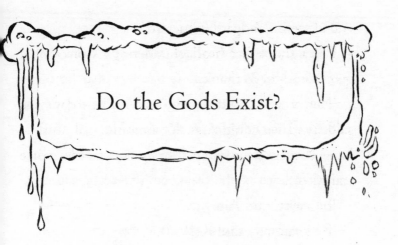

Do the Gods Exist?

BBC Breaking News

The age old question: do the Gods exist? has just been answered – maybe.

It's been announced today that the Gods have been hiding here in plain sight. After being absent for millennia, Woden, Thor and Freyja have revealed themselves in hurricane-shattered London. Yes, that's Woden, the former *FAME: Make Me a Star* winner, Thor the celebrated footballer, and supermodel Freyja. They were joined at a sparsely attended news conference by other Gods, including Njord, Frey, Tyr, Sif, Hermod, Frigg, Idunn, Loki and Heimdall.

When asked why they were revealing

themselves now, Woden the All-Father gave a cryptic reply: 'We have saved you from the melting ice. But next time bad luck may be on your side. Let those who can, achieve glory before the ending of life in this world.'

Then, in an attempt to allay doubts, the All-Father, Lord of the Slain, led a select group of journalists to Highgate Cemetery, where he used charms to raise the dead from their grave mounds. One bearded spectre rose from Karl Marx's mound and asked: 'Is capitalism dead yet?' before sinking back into the ground. The miracle has been posted on YouTube and has already had 17 million views, though others have been quick to condemn what TV magician Knut Brown called 'a cheap stunt'.

Their spokeswoman Veronica Horsley said: 'The great, almighty and immortal Gods have decided that the time was once again right for their worshippers to see them briefly face to face before they return to their heavenly home in Asgard. All-night vigils are being held at Fanes throughout the world to celebrate.'

Not everyone has reacted with favour.

The Archpriest of York issued a statement: 'I look forward to having an audience with the Gods and confirming they are indeed who they say they are.' The Lord High Priestess in Copenhagen has declined to comment.

London Priestess Clare Raven has been besieged by reporters since it was discovered that the Gods lived with her for a few days when they arrived incognito.

'I'm afraid I didn't recognise them at first but they were very well disguised,' said the Priestess. 'However, I was humbled to be their first port of call and glad to show them what hospitality I could.'

When asked what it was like having the Gods in her home, the Priestess said she would not be adding to her statement and invited the journalists to join her for evening worship.

Richard Dawkins writes: 'I don't believe it,' see page 7.

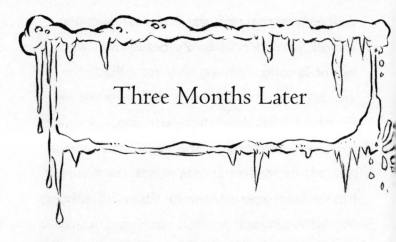

Three Months Later

Freya was on the 259 bus to school. Everywhere she looked there were cranes and skips and yellow-hatted workmen repairing shattered buildings and clearing the last of the storm damage.

She leaned over her friend Emily's shoulder as Emily goggled at the cover of *ICE* magazine.

FREYJA
WHY PLUMP IS THE NEW THIN

Big girls rule now that fashion goddess Freyja leads the pack! Model agencies have dumped all skinny girls who refuse to gain two stone, in an effort to copy the new beauty standard pioneered by Nordic goddess Freyja. With fashion designers

> now only hiring girls sized 16 and over, the
> catwalk revolution in female beauty shows no
> sign of stopping.

Well, that's something at least, thought Freya, flipping to a double-page spread: MEET THE NEW MODELS JOSTLING FOR FREYJA'S CROWN

Her phone vibrated. Veronica. What did *she* want? Since the Gods had returned to Asgard, Veronica had vanished from her life.

'Ah, Freya, I have the most *thrilling* news,' said Veronica, as if they had just spoken yesterday. 'Just what you've always wanted.' Freya could picture Veronica at her desk, checking emails and flicking through newspapers while she talked. 'I've had a call from the producers of *FAME: Make Me a Star* and they want YOU on next year's programme. Yes, you. Isn't that exciting? You're sure to be a huge favourite with the public, and that will vastly increase the money we can get when we sell your story. You'll be famous, honey. Famous. Famous. Famous. What a back story you have: *everyone* will vote for you. Freya? Are you there, Freya?'

Freya was silent.

'I'm not surprised you're speechless, darling. Do you need a moment to think?' said Veronica. 'Don't take too long – an offer like this comes—'

'No,' said Freya. 'I've thought. I don't need worshippers. I don't want anyone's vote. I'm fine as I am.'

Acknowledgements

All writers get stuck, and all writers need good advisers. I'm particularly fortunate in having so many great ones. I'd like to thank my lovely writer friends Joanna Briscoe, Steven Butler, Cressida Cowell, Joanne Harris, Meg Rosoff and Owen Sheers for their generous encouragement, support, and emergency consultations. I'd especially like to thank Steven for his gleeful help with the battle scenes.

I'd also like to thank Dr Emily Lethbridge for taking time out from poring over Norse manuscripts and hurtling down Icelandic crevasses for our many breakfast meetings. And no book ever happens without my agent, Rosemary Sandberg, and the home team, Joshua Stamp-Simon, Martin Stamp, and Shanti.

The amazing people at Profile and Faber – Andrew Franklin, Niamh Murray, Cecily Gayford, Stephen Page, Catherine Daly, Donna Payne, Lucie Ewin (who let me choose the typeface!), Laura Smythe, Leah Thaxton, Rebecca Lee, Rachel Alexander, Susan Holmes and Diana Broccardo make writing a joy, as does working with my brilliant illustrator, Adam Stower.

Three books I found particularly helpful while writing *The Lost Gods* were H.R. Ellis Davidson's *Gods and Myths of Northern Europe*; Andy Orchard's *Dictionary of Norse Myth and Legend*; and Gavin Esler's *Lessons From the Top*.

It's always more wonderful to have written than to write, but I'd like to thank Sally Gardner for reminding me about the value of the journey, whatever the outcome.